T0082688

SHADES OF COLOR AND *Music*

ADRIANA DARDAN

authorHOUSE

AuthorHouse™
1663 Liberty Drive
Bloomington, IN 47403
www.authorhouse.com
Phone: 833-262-8899

Published by AuthorHouse 09/02/2021

ISBN: 978-1-6655-3678-3 (sc)
ISBN: 978-1-6655-3677-6 (e)

Contents

Dedicated vii

Foreword ix

Chapter 1: In the beginning 1

Chapter 2: Later on 66

Chapter 3: Afterward 99

Dedicated

To Edna

Adriana Dardan

Foreword

Shades also called *nuances* are everywhere, real or fictitious, with interpretations of subtle differences in the expression of contours, colors and sounds, or in abstract denominations such as in the meaning of thoughts and feelings. Imagination takes over, amplifies them, multiplies them, and applies them in painting, music, and storytelling, or in every preconceived activity.

Shades are extended on a large scale, from the most faded tones to the most accentuated expressions, and we choose the ones that match the refinement significance of what we think and feel. The nuances of thoughts and feelings are reflected in the expression of the face, in speech, and in behavior; we analyze the subtle graduations of those that we consider most appropriate and which are followed by all the actions resulted from the choices and decisions we make.

Without real and imaginary nuances in all aspects, life would not be the magnificent splendor as it is.

Adriana Dardan

Chapter 1

In the beginning

It was a cold, very early October morning, with heavy rain that has covered the streets and houses of the village during the night, leaving behind puddles and mud over which it was difficult to pass. The faint light bulbs on the streets could only emit a glimmer that was barely visible through the fog and the torrential rain, but at that hour, the streets were deserted and the people had not yet woken up. A silhouette looking more like a shadow in the fog, wrapped in a raincoat, hurried to the convent on the edge of the village, trying in vain to avoid the potholes and mud that dripped at every step. Under the raincoat, the enigmatic figure hid a basket trying to protect it from the torrent of rain, covering it with both arms. From the features of the face, hidden under the hood, one could notice that she was a young girl no older than about fifteen years. Reaching the edge of the stairs, the girl uncovered the basket she had kept hidden and in which was a package wrapped in pieces of thick cloth.

On top, it was attached with a safety pin, a note in which it was written: *"Her name is Edna, she is six months old, and she has no one to raise her. Please take care of her, forgive me, and pray for us"*. She left the basket under the dim light, rang the bell, went down the stairs, hurried in the opposite direction, and hid around the corner of the building, waiting for the convent door to open. Heavy tears mixed with raindrops ran down her face without her trying to stop them.

The convent building was surrounded by about two acres of arable land and was occupied by twelve nuns of French origin. They received stipends from dioceses and donations, but usually they were self-sufficient and had a satisfactory livelihood by procuring their food mainly from the vegetables they grew. Those, supplemented by a few hens that produced eggs, and two cows as a source of dairy food were a sufficient means of subsistence; they made their own clothes, sewing, and knitting, by helping each other like in everything else they did. The nuns addressed each other with the term *Soeur* and the head of the religious house was addressed as *Révérend Mère*. However, because the convent which was named *Saint Matthieu* was located on the outskirts of the village where the population spoke only English, the nuns complied with the situation, and addressed each other with the term

Sister and their leader was addressed as *Reverend Mother*. They spoke French among each other but also had conversational fluency in English.

That morning a nun about eighteen years of age, named Sister Agnes, opened the door at the sound of the bell. She looked around in surprise and suddenly noticed the basket under the eaves. When she saw the baby still sleeping, somehow, she became frightened, and then she made the sign of the cross on him, hurriedly grabbed the basket, and ran with it inside the house. It was a little past four o'clock, the nuns had not yet woken up, and the surrounding silence was complete. Running with the basket in her arms, Sister Agnes knocked on the superior mother's door and entered the room without waiting for the answer.

"I beg your forgiveness for disturbing you at this hour, Reverend Mother, but this is an emergency situation. I heard the bell, opened the door, and found this basket with the baby inside. I looked carefully around but saw nobody, so I took it inside and rushed to your room."

Mother Superior, by her name *Marie*, jumped out of bed, in amazement lifted the baby from the basket, and read with some difficulty the note attached and written in a hurry.

"You are forgiven Sister Agnes; this is indeed an emergency and not a small one. Today we will shorten the morning prayers. Go and wake up all the sisters and gather them in the dining room. Ten minutes! Hurry up!"

With the baby in her arms, she knelt down, said a prayer, and bowed to the cross above the bed. Then she left the room and headed to the dining room where all the nuns were already gathered, anxiously awaiting the explanation of that urgent meeting. At the sight of the baby, everyone exclaimed perplexity and concern. As explicitly as possible, Mother Superior described in front of them the event that took place that morning.

"Her name is *Edna* and she is only six months old. We still don't know how we will solve this situation, but for now, we have to take care of this baby girl and take care of her as much as is achievable. First, Sister Agnes and Sister Colette will go to the village and buy everything a baby needs to be well cared for. Take money out of the cash box and take the car. Sister Rose, find a crate in the garage and temporarily arrange a crib that you will place in Sister Agnes' room with whom the baby will stay. All the other nuns will be nearby and especially helpful in making some changes of clothes from the materials they will find at hand."

The baby started crying.

"She is probably hungry and she needs to be changed", Mother Superior added. "Until we have the necessities bought from the village, Sister Leonie, find a possibility to feed this baby with warm milk; Sister Eugenie, improvise some diapers and some clothes. I have to report to the authorities about this baby and follow the instructions I'll receive. This will take probably some time and we all need patience and practice our usual obedience. This meeting is ended."

In those neighborhoods, the highest authority was Sheriff Davis. At a suitable time, Mother Superior called him on the phone and invited him to come to the convent for an urgent problem. The sheriff came around noon, listened intently to the whole story, read the note found with the baby, and after a few moments of thought said his opinion:

"We don't have many choices, Reverend Mother. First of all, it is very difficult and almost impossible to find the mother of this child. No doubt, she came from afar to leave her baby on the steps of the convent, and disappeared without a trace. Secondly, the adoption of the baby by someone from the village is excluded, considering that all the families here have more children than they can handle. One of the possibilities would be to go to the orphanage in the city, and those out there might find a family to adopt the baby at this young age or later when she grows up. Another possibility would be for her to stay here at the convent and be raised until a certain age when she will be able to support herself. I do not see any other feasible prospect and it is up to you to decide which choice you think is more correct. However, before the decision you will take, the baby must be declared to the Civil Registration Service, regardless of where the birth took place, in order to be recognized by law. In this regard, you have to give the baby a surname and then you can ask for a birth certificate at the County Record. After that, she has to undergo a medical examination at the city hospital to see what her health condition is. Only after all these formalities will be completed, you will be able to make a choice and take a decision that you will consider appropriate. I'll be happy to accompany you or the sister in charge, everywhere in the places I mentioned."

"Thank you Sheriff Davis for all the information you gave me. I'll go with you."

"Very well then. We have to be in the city when the offices open. Tomorrow morning at seven o'clock, I'll come over and pick you up. Good day now, Reverend Mother."

He left and she went to her room with her mind full of heavy thoughts. Kneeling before the cross, she started praying; after a while, she rose on her feet and called Sister Agnes.

"Summon a meeting with all the sisters to be in the dining room half hour from now."

Once there, she gave them a brief description about what the sheriff told her. The nuns looked surprised, but they were not allowed to speak unless addressed, and she didn't ask their opinion. At the end of the meeting, Mother Superior said:

"Tomorrow I'll go to the city with the sheriff and meantime you all will follow your schedule as everyday. Until I'll be back, Sister Catherine will be in charge."

The next morning, the sheriff and Mother Superior holding the baby in her arms set off for the city. In a few hours, they solved all the problems successfully. The baby-girl proved to be in full health and the doctor recommended everything necessary for her normal further development. When asked about the surname of the child at the Registration Service, Mother Superior had a moment of hesitation and then she thought that since the name of the convent was *Saint Mathieu*, she chose for Edna the surname *Mathis.* Regarding the birthday, considering that she was found at the beginning of October with a mention in the note left that she was six months old, her birthday was established as being at the beginning of May.

On the way back, Mother Superior addressed the sheriff, whispering:

"I made the decision to keep the baby with us and upbringing it the best we can. None of us knows how to raise a child, but we'll go slowly, step by step and orient ourselves according to its needs. I chose this solution because I found it the most suitable, from all I had at my disposal."

"With your consent, Reverend Mother, allow me to suggest that my wife who is also a teacher could be of great help to you. We have four children and she has a lot of experience in this issue. I'm sure she will be happy to help you."

"Thank you very much Sheriff Davis, indeed, your wife's experience could help us a lot and I appreciate very much the proposal you made to me."

At the sound of the approaching car, all the sisters ran to the front door eagerly awaiting the news. Mother Superior said goodbye to the sheriff, thanking him for his assistance, and entered the building with the baby in her arms.

"Everyone in the dining room for a short meeting!"

All the sisters hurried to listen without hiding the curiosity that could be seen on their faces, but without asking any questions. In a few words, Mother Superior described the results obtained that morning, adding:

"I made the decision for Edna to stay with us and be raised according to the regulations of our congregation. My decision was based on the fact that the number of nuns is declining day by day and there are no candidates to appear from the outside world. Until the age of four, she will grow up as a child like in any family; she will be able to speak consistently in both French and English; she will learn to keep herself clean; she will have time to learn useful games, and she will get used to obedience. In that period, she will share the room with Sister Agnes. By turn, each one of you will skip the Sunday service and stay with her. She will gradually learn the simple and short prayers, said at the time indicated to her, and she will get used to kneeling without complaining; she will begin attending Sunday service after the age of four; also, at that age, she will be assigned the room at the end of the corridor where the cleaning stuff is now stored and which will be moved to the shed. At school age, she will be enrolled in the village middle school, which has eight grades and I consider that those are enough for her education; she will be fourteen at graduation. After that, she will be assigned to a workplace, and will follow the novitiate, which as you know, is the period of apostolic preparation in our religious order before taking the oath. That being said, the meeting is over and you all go back to work!"

Time passed without new incidents and Edna grew up under the supervision of Sister Agnes who proved a special attachment to her. The other nuns were drawn to the sweetness of that child, but Mother Superior who had forbidden any intention of pampering her restricted their proximity to her. The child had to be raised according to the strict regulations of the religious order. Even so, every night before bed, Sister Agnes took the baby in her arms and sang her a lullaby she remembered from her childhood, or whispered to her so that she would not be heard outside the room, a story remembered from her mother. She kissed the baby's forehead and Edna smiled. Her maternal instincts hidden deep in her soul rose to tears; she wished this baby she loved so much would be hers.

The sheriff's wife came from time to time and her advice was very helpful, especially when none of the nuns knew much about raising children.

By the time Edna was two years old, she had become restless, running down the corridors, and slipping out the back door, if unattended. She was curious about everything she saw, and could speak in a mixed language of English and French that only Sister Agnes could understand. When another nun approached her, she smiled and pulled her skirt, trying a kind of communication that she needed, but which remained unanswered. Edna had begun to develop a very friendly character, but the restrictions in which she was constrained to grow drowned out any enthusiasm and any expression of her feelings, forcing her to take refuge in shyness combined with fear. She was very attached to Sister Agnes, but she had learned that she was not allowed to show her feelings when other nuns were present, and especially Mother Superior, whom Edna understood without being told that she had to avoid. She did not have toys like all children have, but only a few figurines carved in wood by the handyman who helped the sisters and who received approval to give them to the child. From time to time, did Sister Agnes tell her a story that Edna received with great pleasure and memorized. When she was alone she tried to repeat it in front of the figurines she was talking with and enriched her language that no one cared about if it was clear or confusing.

Gradually, with the passing of time, her personality began to develop between the strict environment in which she lived and her imagination full of questions that she was not allowed to ask in order to find answers.

The sheriff's wife, who came from time to time and gave advice, had received approval and brought her some coloring books and some pencils accompanied by a drawing sketchbook with white sheets. Edna had a great pleasure in following the contours of the figures in the books and coloring them. Then, she tried to copy them from memory to her sketchbook, attempting to give the lines as much accuracy as possible. When she showed Sister Agnes her drawings, she was astonished and worried at the same time:

"Don't spend too much time on these. Be careful and repeat the prayers I have taught you because you need them more than knowing how to draw."

Edna already knew what she had to do, and she replied confidently:

"Yes, Sister Agnes, I will do as you say."

However, in her mind, the wording of the answer was completely different: (I will say as few prayers as possible and draw as much as I like, without asking your or others' permission.)

At the age of four, Edna was moved from the room she shared with Sister Agnes to a very small chamber at the end of the corridor with only a tiny bed and some poor furniture. A crucifix above the bed was the only ornament on the whitewashed walls of the room. At that age she was dressed in a long, gray dress, and was forced to wear a white cap on her head.

On the first night when she had to sleep alone in her room, Edna was frightened and said to Sister Agnes:

"I'm afraid to be alone at night in the dark and I want to be with you as before."

"It's not the way you or I want it to be, and it's hard for me also to be separated from you after we've been together since you were a baby. However, it is the order given by the superior mother, and if we do not obey, we will both be punished. Don't be afraid of the dark or any other danger around you. I'll stay with you in your room until you fall asleep, and you'll be all right. What do you say?"

"I'll try to be obedient, if you stay with me until I fall asleep."

When bedtime came, Sister Agnes sat down on the chair by Edna's bed, waiting for the little girl to fall asleep. After a while, she slowly left the room without waking her. She reached her room, and let out a deep sigh of sadness. When she was almost asleep, she heard a light knock on the door. Sister

Agnes rushed and opened the door, and found herself with Edna in her arms, clinging to her chest. She trembled, cried, and could only whisper:

"I can't sleep there. I'm scared."

"Stay here now, but tomorrow you will try to sleep in your room. You have to get used to it if you don't want to be punished and drag me into punishment also. Think about me, too."

Edna smiled and kissed her on both cheeks.

A few nights were repeated in the same way. Eventually, Edna relented and became convinced that she should not be afraid of darkness or imagined threats.

Gradually, Sister Agnes had to teach her longer, but simple prayers that Edna had to say three times daily at the assigned time, kneeling before the crucifix, and without complaining. The poor child had no idea why she was constrained by those rules which, if she did not obey, she was punished by kneeling and facing the wall for at least half an hour. When she asked about the meaning of those prayers, one of the nuns tried to clarify:

"It is the way in which man expresses his request for forgiveness of sins to the Almighty God who created the world. You must show humility and a desire to be forgiven for your sins, and you must obey the rules of our religion without commenting or complaining. If you do not pray, your sins will not be forgiven and you will burn in hell."

"What is hell?"

"The place where sinners are sent to be burned alive."

"What sins I have committed? I want to know to pray for their forgiveness."

"No one knows what sins has committed because they are hidden and only God knows them. No one is clean and without sin, and everyone must pray to be forgiven."

Edna did not insist on further explanations; her fear of being burned in hell was imprinted on her mind enough to make her determined to be as obedient as she could be. However, many times she forgot her obligations and took the liberty of behaving as her personality developed. When she was allowed free activity for an hour every day, she really enjoyed sitting outside in the middle of nature and drawing what she saw around her: trees, birds, flowers and even the silhouettes of the nuns working in the fields. She often liked to sit near the fence and watch people pass by or children playing ball on the street. She tried to memorize their figures, gestures, clothing, and the way they moved; then she drew from memory all the images that had imprinted themselves on her mind. In those moments, she was very happy and completely forgot that she was in a monastery where she had to listen, be humble, and say prayers. In those moments, she completely forgot about hell and the fact that she could be burned for her sins. She was in a world of her own where she could let go of her imagination, which no one could control or stop. Even if the features of people she drew were not exactly correct, one could easily recognize the personages in her drawings and her outstanding talent. Back in her room, she hid the sketchbook under the mattress so she wouldn't be scolded if it was found. She could neither read nor write, and she would have very much liked to learn so that she could discover novelties from storybooks. One day, she took her courage and addressed her wish to Sister Agnes:

"We must ask permission from Mother Superior and if she allows, I will fulfill your wish."

Sister Agnes found a time when Mother Superior was in a calm mood, and expressed what Edna desired.

"It's a little early for her to read and write, but sometimes we have to give her a treat just to encourage her to commit to rules and obligations. You are allowed to fulfill her wish."

At Sister Agnes's call, Mrs. Davis was kind enough to help and brought Edna a book with exercises of the alphabet, a few storybooks, sketchbooks, and pencils, while giving her useful advices in the same time. They were all three in Edna's room when someone called Sister Agnes, who went out for a few minutes. Edna took the opportunity to speak after taking her sketchbook with the drawings hidden under the mattress:

"Mrs. Davis, please keep my sketchbook until I can get it back. I am afraid that if any of the sisters finds it, she will report me to the superior mother and I will be punished. Can you do this for me?"

"With great pleasure, Edna. Your secret is safe with me."

She took the sketchbook and put it in the briefcase she came with. At that moment, Sister Agnes appeared in the room.

"Edna, say thanks to Mrs. Davis for her kindness in responding to our request. For my part, I thank you also, and I hope for good results."

"Thank you very much, Mrs. Davis, for all you have done for me," Edna added.

"The joy is mine, especially since I'm a school teacher and Edna will be my student."

Mrs. Davis went home with many thoughts that had begun to bother her. The sheriff had just come for lunch and set the table waiting for his wife. She handed him the sketchbook with Edna's drawings:

"George, look at this."

He looked intently at every page and drawing, while amazement grew on his face.

"Did Edna do this?"

"Yes, Edna did this secretly so as not to be punished."

"I'm just amazed. You know what I think, Magda? I think, this little girl will never be a nun."

"I think so too, George."

Not so long after, Edna learned to read and write easily and with great pleasure. She could follow with understanding and without difficulty the development of the action and the composition of the characters in her storybooks; the satisfaction she had could not be described in simple words. She managed to completely detach herself from the entourage in which she lived and she was able to participate with all enthusiasm in the development of the action and the transformations that the characters in the story went through. She liked to talk to each character and express her approving or disapproving opinion about everyone's action and attitude. Moreover, Edna drew in her sketchbook the characters from the story, this time writing the name of each one next to the picture represented. Just like before, she hid the sketchbook with her drawings under the mattress, so that she wouldn't be scolded if it was found. Edna would have liked to show her drawings to Sister Agnes, but her instinct for prudence proved to be greater. She thought that if the superior mother might find out, they will both be punished and they will be separated from each other.

One morning, the superior mother called sister Agnes to her office and told her to bring Edna with one of her storybooks. There, she subjected the girl to a reading and writing examination, after which she looked satisfied, but didn't say a word. Next, she took a book off the shelf in French and examined her again carefully. It was the first time that Edna was faced with a text in French, but she easily managed to please the superior mother, who, without saying a word of praise, was limited to a few new duties that Edna had to perform from then on:

"Starting tomorrow you are assigned to help the sister in the kitchen with washing dishes. Also, starting this Sunday, you will attend the church service, sitting next to Sister Agnes. You will not make a move, you will not talk, and you will read the prayers together with the sisters. Is this all clear for you?"

"Yes, Reverend Mother, everything is clear."

"You can go now."

Edna left the office and Sister Agnes remained behind, showing great surprise on her face.

"Do you have something to say?", the superior mother asked.

"With all due respect, Reverend Mother, I think Edna is far too young for the obligations you mentioned. No nun began her novitiate at such a young age. Edna is barely a child who needs free time, to play, and to learn what a child her age can assimilate. She is not yet old enough to work and read the book of prayers from which she will certainly not understand anything. "

"That's what I decided and that's how it will be. You can retire now."

Sister Agnes left the room with her soul full of anxiety and with many confused thoughts seeking release.

The next day, Edna has been taken to the kitchen by Sister Agnes and met Sister Colette who was in charge there. That one gave Edna a short lesson about washing dishes, gave her an apron and, as a start, some small plates and cups. Edna started her new assignment with big care not to break anything and with tears in her eyes longing for her beloved books and drawings. When back to her room, she was supposed to read prayers, which she tried hard to understand at least some of the content, but she was unable even to follow the words. After few minutes, she fell asleep and Sister Agnes found her lying on the floor. She woke her up, dressed her for the night, and put her to bed.

"Good night sweet angel", she said, but Edna was already asleep.

The next few days were the same as the first, with no difference from one to another and with no improvement in little Edna's life. Everything for her has become monotonous, cumbersome, uninteresting, and lacking in perspective. A little revitalization appeared on Sundays when she had to attend religious service.

The church was about two hundred yards from the main building and was large enough to accommodate the villagers who usually came to the religious service. On the floor was the altar facing the rows of benches on which were prayer books arranged for the parishioners. At the top was a balcony, where the nuns sat, and in one corner was a small organ where Sister Catherine played. She was older than the other nuns and had a higher education than the others. A priest from the city came every Sunday and performed the religious service.

On that first Sunday when Edna attended the service, she sat down next to Sister Agnes as the superior mother had decided. All the nuns were already in place when the parishioners began to arrive and fill the church. At first, Edna was curious and looked at the people coming in, then she had to pay attention to what was going on. After everyone sat down on the benches, the priest came out of the altar and began the service. He started with a prayer, and then began to read from a voluminous book; after that the sisters while kneeled, read prayers with the priest, then the whole congregation sang prayers accompanied on the organ. Next, many of the same instances were repeated, and almost two hours had passed when little Edna whispered to Sister Agnes:

"I am tired of being kneeled for so long, and I do not understand a word of what the priest says, and not a word of what I have to read from this book. I no longer want to be here!"

"Be quiet, and wait a little, it's almost done."

"I can't, and I won't!"

She threw the prayer book on the floor, and run outside. A little commotion could be sensed by everyone, but no big attention was given to the incident. Sister Agnes got up slowly and went outside after Edna; she found her near the fence crying with sobs. Without saying a word, she took the little girl in her arms, trying to calm her down. She took her to her room and put her to bed, hoping that Edna would calm down. Sister Agnes sat on the chair and began to read from the prayer book. Edna fell asleep with difficulty but was agitated and had nightmares. Sister Agnes caressed her forehead and sang more like whispering a lullaby until Edna calmed down. The sisters had not yet come, because after the religious service they had to receive the Holy Communion as every Sunday. Sitting in the chair with her prayer book open, Sister Agnes noticed a corner of Edna's sketchbook sticking out from under the mattress. She didn't take it out even though she was curious, and she pushed it deeper inside so that it wouldn't be noticed. She thought that if Edna felt the need to talk, she would tell her without asking why she kept hidden her sketchbook. After about an hour, she heard footsteps in the corridor, signifying that the sisters had returned from church. The door opened and the superior mother appeared in the doorway:

"How is she and why did she make such a turmoil?"

"She is asleep, but she cried a lot because she was exhausted from being kneeled for so long. I barely calmed her down because she was very distressed."

"When she wakes up, bring her to the office to teach her a behavior lesson."

Without another word, she turned and left.

Edna woke up late in the afternoon, but she was calmer and happy when she saw Sister Agnes sitting next to her.

"I slept a lot and I'm very sorry I bothered you. I don't know what happened to me but I felt pain all over my body and the need to cry. Can you forgive me?"

"You did nothing wrong to me to ask forgiveness. It wasn't your fault at all. However, I give you some advice and remember what I say. The superior mother asked me to bring you to the office to scold you and to punish you for your behavior. I advise you when you get in front of her, before she starts talking, get on your knees, and ask for forgiveness, promising not to repeat what you did. Otherwise, she will scold you and punish you severely. You understand?"

"I understand Sister Agnes, and I'll do as you advised me. Thank you from the bottom of my heart for taking care of me and always protecting me."

Without waiting for a comment, Edna kissed her on both cheeks lovingly. She hesitated one moment, then made a decision and said:

"I have great confidence in you and I would very much like to share with you something which is dear to me. Can you keep it a secret?"

"You know that you can trust me. Your secret will be safe with me."

Edna took the sketchbook out from under the mattress and handed it to Sister Agnes. She opened it and was greatly surprised.

"It is admirable what you drew here; I'm amazed by what I see. The talent you prove is unimaginable for your age. I really appreciate that you trust me and you revealed your secret to me. Keep the sketchbook under the mattress for any eventuality. I congratulate you not only for your talent but also for your desire to work on your drawings. Keep going but be very careful not to be discovered, or we both we'll be punished. Let's go now."

The bond between them became even stronger.

Arriving at the superior mother's office, Sister Agnes knocked softly on the door.

"Come in."

Edna went in first and heard the command:

"Sit down!"

Instead of complying, Edna walked around the desk and shyly approached the superior mother. She knelt with her head bowed, palms close as in prayer, and carried out her greatest performance:

"I beg your forgiveness, Reverend Mother, for my turbulent behavior in the church. I promise it will never happen again and I beg you from the bottom of my heart to forgive me."

Mother Superior was surprised and thought that maybe she had pushed that child too far. She had prepared a harsh admonishment plan and a new way to punish her, but suddenly everything she had planned was scattered like under a magic sign. In a calm voice she replied:

"I forgive you this time. I appreciate your attitude and the humility you show. I have decided that you will continue to work in the kitchen as before, and at the Sunday religious service, you will be next to Sister Agnes, not kneeling, but sitting on the bench. You will be present at the religious service as a spectator and not as a participant; you will observe the whole ceremony and you will gradually learn how it takes place. You can go now."

"Thank you Reverend Mother."

"Go!"

Outside the office, they both smiled at each other. They were hungry because neither of them had eaten since the day before, went to the kitchen, and ate to their heart's content.

"I have to go back to work but you can stay outside and enjoy the fresh air. Today you don't need to work in the kitchen. Until dinner, walk on the grass or play or get a book and read. You have plenty of time to refresh yourself. Bye now, my sweet angel."

"I wish my name was Alice as the little girl in my favorite story, who was protected by a fairy sent by an angel from heaven. You are like the fairy who protects me and I am sure you were sent by an angel from heaven. Bye, my beloved fairy."

Edna took a storybook and sat on the grass trying to read and imagining the characters like she usually did. However, there were many unanswered questions in her mind, thinking about what happened that morning. She recapitulated each segment of what occurred, and concluded that she was not guilty. It all came out unfavorably only because she was forced to follow the activity in the church from which she understood nothing; being forced to kneel, she got tired and her body was full of pain she could no longer bear. She had to run outside to alleviate her suffering and not because she was against the rules and wanted to disobey them. She didn't have to apologize for what she was not guilty. Rather she should have explained to the superior mother what had been true and force her to accept the truth. Nevertheless, it seemed that things could not go according to what happened in reality. Sister Agnes advised her to apologize, probably because it was the only way she could escape punishment. She did so and obtained peace, but in her mind was the confusion between lie and truth, and seemed to be no choice when life was in danger. Edna was convinced she was not guilty and had to lie by apologizing, just so she wouldn't be severely punished. With this conclusion, she felt very satisfied with her reasoning. That day, Edna learned an important constituent in the struggle for survival: the need to use hypocrisy whenever she was threatened with danger. She didn't know the word but she understood the power of it on which about everything seemed to be based in that convent.

The next day Edna returned to her work in the kitchen. She got along very well with Sister Colette, who appreciated her for her diligence and friendly attitude. It was a cold day with heavy rain flowing like a curtain. Sister Colette told Edna to bring some cleaning solutions from the shed, but she didn't have time to tell her to pay attention to the rain and take her rain cloak, because Edna had already gone outside and was hurrying to the shed. When she returned to the kitchen, she was all wet and shivering. Sister Colette sent her to her room telling her to change her clothes and stay there until dinner because the kitchen work was almost done. Edna ran to her room and threw herself on the bed shivering from the cold and trying to warm herself under the blanket. At dinnertime, she did not get out of bed and did not go to the table because she felt weak, and had not recovered from shivering. Noticing that she was late, Sister Agnes ran to see what happened and immediately realized that Edna had fallen ill, was not feeling well at all, and barely could breathe. She touched her forehead and understood that the girl had high fever. She tried to warm her but failed, and from Edna's words, she understood that the girl had been in the rain without a rain cloak and the cold rain penetrated her to the skin. Sister Agnes immediately informed the superior mother who was already at dinner saying the blessing prayer.

"Call the doctor if you think she has high fever."

She got up from the table and came to Edna's room to convince herself that the little girl was ill.

The paramedics arrived in less than half an hour, coming from the city. They checked on Edna, and one of them said:

"She needs medical treatment immediately and we will transport her to the children's hospital in the city. One of the sisters can come with us or follow us by car."

Mother Superior was very quick this time, probably because she was scared.

"Sister Agnes, take the car and go with her. Call me as soon as the doctor will examine her. I'll be in my office."

As soon as they arrived at the hospital, Edna was taken to the emergency room, and a doctor immediately came to examine her. She had fever, was breathing hard, and had begun to cough; two nurses were around her, doing everything the doctor said. An hour later, the doctor approached Sister Agnes, who was waiting anxiously in the hall:

"She has symptoms of pneumonia and we have to keep her hospitalized for a while, when she will have the necessary treatment. Paramedics brought her in time, so I do not foresee complications for now, although she looks malnourished and probably she needs plenty of vitamins and calcium. In this regard, we'll do some tests to make sure about her condition. She also seems to be under a lot of stress, but we'll have to do more tests in this regard also. For now, she receives intravenous fluids and antibiotics, as well as oxygen therapy. You can return to the convent because it is not necessary for you to stay here. I assure you that she has the best care and if you want, you can call tomorrow morning to know how she is. That's all I can tell you for now."

"Thank you doctor. I would like to stay in the waiting room until tomorrow morning and maybe I can see her when she gets up, so she wouldn't be scared in a strange place."

"You can stay, but you cannot get close to her when she gets up. You can see her through the window. Good night."

"One more thing please. May I use the phone to call my superior?"

"It's on the desk. Maybe I should talk to your superior and explain the situation."

Sister Agnes called the superior mother who answered immediately. She told her only a few words and gave the phone to the doctor. After he told her in details about Edna's condition, she only asked:

"When she will be able to come home?"

"I cannot tell you. We have to see how she will progress in recovering; this is all I can say."

Sister Agnes sat in the waiting room all night in an armchair, trying to fall asleep. Early in the morning, a nurse came and brought her a cup of milk with a donut.

"Thank you. Can I see her now? "

"Only through the window. You are not allowed to enter the room."

Sister Agnes approached the window, Edna saw her, waved her hand weakly, and closed her eyes. After a few minutes, Sister Agnes left for the convent, with many heavy thoughts running through her mind.

After ten days, Edna was moved to the recovery room where other three girls about her age were in beds and talked to each other. The doctor came into the room and approached her:

"I'm Doctor James Brennen, and I'm pleased to meet you Edna. How do you feel?"

"I'm feeling better, thank you Doctor James."

"Do you know where you are and why are you here?"

"I was very sick and this is a hospital where sick children are treated."

"Very good, and that's true. Now, tell me something about yourself. What are you doing usually, all day in the convent?"

"I pray three times daily, then I work in the kitchen washing dishes, and one hour I'm allowed outside to read my storybooks, or to draw in my sketchbook, and have some fresh air. If I am disobedient, I am punished by kneeling in the corner facing the wall."

She motioned for him to come closer and whispered:

"I learned a secret from Sister Agnes who is my protective fairy: if I beg forgiveness first, I am no longer punished."

At that moment when Edna mentioned her chore in the kitchen, and about being punished, the doctor opened his mouth and seemed ready to explode, but only said:

"Now, you listen to Nurse Lucy who gives you treatment, make sure that you eat well, and talk to your room mates. I'll come in the afternoon to see you."

He left the room like a thunderstorm and rushed to his office. He called the superior mother at the convent and when he heard her voice, he started yelling like in hell, without any introduction:

"How dare you exploit a four-year-old little girl, forcing her to work, endangering her health and constraining her into mental stress, instead of taking care of her and raising her as any child needs to be raised?! Edna is barely a baby, she is fragile and vulnerable not only physically but also mentally and spiritually. She is malnourished, she is under normal weight for her age, and is scared of any word spoken out loud, meaning she is under constant stress. No social law and no divine law allow such abusive behavior as you have there towards her. Do you call yourself a nun in the service of the Creator? Shame on you!"

"Doctor Brennen, Edna is in the convent and must obey the strict canonical legislation that regulates the life and mission of the Church. She must be prepared for the novitiate to become a nun. She is not abused, she is only directed to learn what is right. That's all."

"Oh, but that's not all! Edna will stay here until I consider that she has all the vital signs restored to normal. She is in your custody and I cannot intervene in this direction; nevertheless, I solemnly promise you that I will act drastically if you continue to mistreat her as before. A member of the social service will come over to the convent and often monitor your behavior and the child's living conditions. One wrong step if you do, I will send the authorities and the social media on your head, and you can be sure that the next day, all your convent and the whole history that happened will be on the front page of every newspaper in the country! I promise a disaster to you all and to your diocese. Good day!"

Edna was fed five times a day in small portions of delicious food that she never tasted before and did not even know that existed. Her clothes were changed often, she was given daily a bath and massage. She was allowed to play in a room where there were many toys, storybooks, and where children between the ages of one and five were recovering. They were constantly supervised by a kindergarten teacher who showed great dedication in the care she had for them. Edna was happy for the first time in her life. Sometimes, instead of playing with the children, she chose to draw. She liked playing a game with numbers and she learned how to count. All the staff loved her for her friendly nature and her behavior, which made her to be loved not only by doctors and nurses, but especially by children. At her age, her traits were well defined and she had become a child of unusual beauty. She had light auburn, wavy hair, almond shaped dark green eyes with long eyelashes, and her skin was like fine porcelain. Her small nose was well-proportionate to the shape of her face, and she had beautifully contoured lips. When she smiled, her whole face suddenly radiated and attracted everyone's admiration. One day she asked Nurse Lucy:

"How do I look like? I've never seen my face."

"You never looked in a mirror?"

"No."

"Then I'll give you one. Here, take this."

She gave her a small mirror and Edna was greatly surprised when she saw her face."

"Is this me?"

"For sure, it's not me. Must be you."

She started moving her mouth, her eyes, then making faces until she burst into laugh.

"I like my face, Nurse Lucy."

"I like it too, Edna. You can keep the mirror."

The first thing she did, was to draw her face next to the other drawings, wrote her name, and had an immensely good feeling. In her sketchbook, she drew about every face she met in the hospital. When doctor Brennen saw his portrait, he was amazed:

"If I didn't know, I would never believed it. Who taught you to draw like that?"

"Nobody. I just draw like I feel. Would you like to have it Doctor James? I can make another drawing of you to keep it for myself."

"I'll be honored Edna to have it, and I'll put it in a frame and keep it on my desk. Thank you for your kindness. Maybe, one day you'll become a celebrity."

In a month Edna had fully recovered, gained weight, her vital signs came to normal, and she was always happy. It was about time to leave the hospital, but Doctor Brennen decided to keep her for a while.

Ever since she had that stormy conversation with the doctor, the superior mother had learned nothing about Edna. One day she called Sister Agnes:

"Go to the hospital and if she recovered, bring her home."

Sister Agnes went to the hospital and spoke with the nurse at the desk. The nurse called Doctor Brennen, who didn't seem surprised to see her. In a detailed description, he told her what Edna's situation was and added:

"She has made great strides in health, but I intend to keep her here to see how she evolves mentally also. It's not the right time for her to leave the hospital. Come after three weeks."

Sister Agnes thanked him warmly and added in a whisper:

"Between you and me, Doctor Brennen, I would like you to keep her here as long as possible. Can I see her now?"

"Certainly. I must say that I have great consideration for you, Sister Agnes. You proved to be good, kind, and understanding to Edna, and she is very fond of you. You can see her now."

A nurse came and led her to the daily room where the children were gathered and playing. When Edna saw Sister Agnes, she rushed straight into her arms.

"I'm so happy to see you, my protective fairy!"

"I am also happy to see you my sweet angel! How are you feeling? I see that you are playing with children and I know that this is a great benefit for you."

"I feel wonderful, and the children are all adorable and we get along very well. Some of them leave, some others come, but we all are good friends. I eat a lot and everything is very tasty because I don't leave anything on the plate. Doctor James checks me twice a day and tells me that I'm healthy. Here's what Nurse Lucy who takes care of me gave me the other day."

Edna took out of her pocket the small mirror she had received and saw her face for the first time. Sister Agnes was thrilled by the unrestrained effusion that Edna was showing. Indeed, without a doubt, the little girl was treated with the best possible care.

Sister Agnes stayed with her for more than two hours, during which time Edna spoke continuously, telling in detail everything that happens there every day. She had also shown her the sketchbook with drawings and Sister Agnes was impressed by the progress Edna made. At the time of departure, they hugged each other with all their heart, promising each other to always think about those two hours they spent together, completely forgetting all the troubles.

Back at the convent, Sister Agnes gave the superior mother a short statement, without details, and especially without any mention of the happy way Edna felt.

"Doctor Brennen told me she had to be kept in the hospital to see if she was completely recovered. Probably other three or four weeks."

The superior mother listened carefully, did not ask any questions, and did not utter a word. Only she could tell what was going on in her mind.

Meantime, Sister Agnes went to Edna's room, kneeled in front of her bed, and raised a warm prayer to Lord Creator, thanking Him for the little girl's recovery, and begging him to keep her safe.

After three weeks, Dr. Brennen had to let Edna go. Sister Agnes came in the morning and asked to speak to him. In his office, he invited her to sit down for a long conversation. He showed her four pages of instructions that had to be followed precisely and that included the feeding program and diet, the supplementation with vitamins and minerals, the activity program, and the rest periods. Every month Edna had to come for a check-up to see her health. A social worker had to visit her every two weeks and present a detailed report to the doctor about the conditions in which Edna was living. A precise clause was the categorical prohibition for Edna from being subjected to any kind of physical labor. If his orders are not strictly obeyed, serious repercussions will follow.

When asked by the doctor, Sister Agnes replied that she understood everything and would hand over the instructions to the superior mother. On the doctor's table were bottles of vitamins, minerals, and dietary supplements prepared for Edna. It was also prepared for her a suitcase with new clothes and a backpack with books, sketchbooks, and pencils.

After the discussion, the doctor called the nurse and told her to bring Edna. When she saw Sister Agnes, the little girl threw herself into her arms.

"I'm so happy to see you my protective fairy!"

"I'm happy too, my sweet angel, but it's time to take you home."

Edna took turns looking at her and the doctor, then addressed them both:

"I do not want to go back there. For the first time in my life, I was happy here and I knew what it means to have a home. I don't want to go back to where suffering is always there for me. Doctor James, please don't let me go."

The doctor answered with emotion in his voice:

"Edna, as much as I would like, I cannot keep you here, because the hospital has rules that have to be followed. If I break them, the authorities can punish me and even send me to jail. Would you accept that something like that happens to me?"

"Oh no, Doctor James! I rather go there than causing trouble for you and make you suffer. I want you to always love me, do you?"

"I do love you Edna very much, and I thank you for understanding me. Now, let me tell you something that might please you: your lifestyle will change there completely. You'll not be allowed to work in the kitchen anymore or somewhere else; only if you want, and I specify, only if you have the desire, you can help the sisters with light tasks that do not require physical effort or stress; it's your choice;

a social worker, that is someone who will check on you, will come over and visit you often, and she will report directly to me about your living conditions and about your activities; you'll not have to pray three times daily, but only once before going to bed, and you'll never be punished again; if you want, you can attend the Sunday service, and I suggest you to do that, but only for as long as you don't get tired; you'll eat special meals which will be cooked only for you; you'll not wear the long gray dress, but only the clothes prepared for you in this suitcase and that you liked here; you'll have all the time during the day to spend the way you wish; in this backpack are books, sketchbooks and pencils for you to enjoy. What do you think about these changes?"

"I'm very pleased Doctor James, and I don't know what to say, except that I can deal very well with this kind of my new life. I'm ready to go back to the convent."

Edna bit farewell to all those who cared for her and loved her in that place she called *Home.*

On the way to the convent, she asked Sister Agnes:

"Do you think the superior mother will accept Dr. James' orders?"

"I don't know, but I hope she will accept them. We'll see, and you don't have to worry."

In fact, Sister Agnes was very worried about. However, she knew nothing of the stormy conversation between the doctor and the superior mother, so she did not know about the doctor's threats and the consequences that would follow if his orders were not carried out.

Arriving at the convent, Sister Agnes took the luggage and they both went to Edna's room:

"Unpack everything and find a suitable place for whatever is in the luggage. Stay in the room; I'll go to see the superior mother and give her the doctor's instructions. When I return, we will talk about what we have to do."

Mother Superior was in her office writing some papers. Sister Agnes knocked on the door and entered without being called.

"Edna is in her room, and these are Dr. Brennen's instructions for further treatment."

The superior mother took the sheets of paper, gave them a brief look, and said nothing about them, but added:

"You will make sure that everything is fulfilled, and you will continue to take care of Edna. Our supplier in the village will provide all the products recommended by the doctor for her nourishment. Ask the cook to prepare her meals as prescribed, and she will eat in her room. You can leave now. "

Sister Agnes expected a stormy reaction, but it didn't come, because the superior mother had memorized every threat posed by the doctor in the discussion she had with him; Sister Agnes had no way of knowing, but she was glad that the storm she had been waiting for had not broken out. She returned to Edna's room, told her about the superior mother's reaction, and then asked her:

"Are you going to attend this coming Sunday the holy service?"

"Yes."

"Then you'll have to wear the long gray dress and the white cap."

"I will. You know what I think?"

"No. Tell me."

"I think that the Lord Creator chose for me to get sick, so that I could go to the hospital and know how different from the convent life is. I've also learned there that people are different, that they love each other and care one about the other. I saw many sick children like me who were treated by nurses and doctors with great care and love the same as I was treated. I learned what happiness is when I knew how much those people loved me and how much I could love them without restrictions. Don't you think that I'm right, Sister Agnes?"

"I think you're right and I think you're very smart, Edna. You're a very sensitive girl and very good in your heart. I think you'll never hurt someone in your life and you'll be always good to everyone."

"I wish I'll be as you described me, and I'll be very pleased with myself, then."

"Good. Now, it's lunch time and you have to eat. After that, you do whatever pleases you, and I'll have to take care of some unfinished task."

After lunch, Edna took her sketchbook and went outside. Sitting on the grass, she decided to make a better drawing of herself. Keeping the mirror in a convenient position, she began to sketch the lines of her face, emphasizing the shades of light and shadow. The attention with which she followed her image in the mirror required more time than ever when she sketched a human figure. She repeated the sketch several times until the drawing became almost exact, which gave her great satisfaction. That day, Edna learned to draw more accurately the features of her face, by giving more importance to the nuances of shadows and light, which she never before observed in details. With each sketch she drew, she noticed that the shades of light and shadow had a different position; they were moving on the face in the mirror, which was something new that she had not noticed in the drawings made before. At her young age Edna begun to show an unusual perception in which the impressions collected by her senses were accurately interpreted in her mind.

When Sister Agnes saw the sketches, she repeated Doctor Brennen's remark:

"If I didn't know, I would never believed it. With every passing day you make big progress, Edna. I'm really amazed."

"Would you like to pose for me and I'll make your portrait?"

"I would love to. Maybe tomorrow you'll do it."

Next day they both went outside and sat under a tree where light and shadow merged in a pleasant combination. It took Edna more than one hour to sketch Sister Agnes' face, but she did a marvelous drawing. She put all her effort and concentrated all her talent in order to finally realize an admirable portrait made with great accuracy. Sister Agnes had tears in her eyes when she saw it. She only could say:

"I have not enough words to express my emotion. Your talent is amazing. May I have this drawing? I'll keep it forever, remembering this day."

"I'm happy that you like it and I'm happy to give it to you so you can remember this day."

Sister Agnes caressed her head, and many thoughts about that little girl started to run through her mind.

The following Sunday, Edna attended the holy service as she said. Her behavior was impeccable; not only did she stand at the whole service even though she was tired at one point, but she joined the sisters' choir, following the songs from the book. The superior mother who observed her was astonished and very delighted.

Time passed by, and in fall, Edna was enrolled in first grade of school; there were fifteen children in class, seven boys and eight girls. Mrs. Davis was very pleased seeing her and said:

"I have to tell you from the beginning that you'll get bored Edna with the teachings in first grade, since your level is much above your classmates."

"Don't worry, Mrs. Davis, I'll be all right. I'm happy to be in school and I'm never bored. There is always something new to learn."

"I appreciate your attitude and indeed, there is always something new to learn."

Each student had received a new backpack with requisites and many storybooks.

Edna befriended her classmates quickly and found many common topics to talk about together. The school was about a half-hour walking distance, and Edna soon learned to walk alone without being accompanied by Sister Agnes. The four hours of class passed quickly and Edna always found something new she didn't know about. She was exempt from many homework assignments, but she had to learn about science and arithmetic, which were interesting for her.

Every day she told Sister Agnes in detail about everything she had done in school, telling her that she liked there very much and she was happy. After finishing her homework, she went outside and read from storybooks, imagining the characters and sometimes drawing them. One day she saw Sister Catherine planting flowers in pots, and approached her:

"May I help you?"

"Of course and thank you for your attention. I like flowers very much and I want to take a few pots to my room. If you want, take these two and come with me."

Edna did as she was told and accompanied her to the room, where Sister Catherine placed the pots on the edge of the window.

"Flowers remind me of places at home. I was born and grew up in Paris where there was a rich vegetation and many flowers."

"Where is Paris? Far away from here?"

"Very far. Have a seat and I'll show you how far is from here."

Sister Catherine was the only nun who was allowed to keep her possessions brought from home, because she donated a large sum of money to the diocese when she joined the convent.

She took a volume from the shelf, opened it in the middle where there was a map of the World.

"Here is the convent where we live, and on the other side is Paris."

"This is very, very far from here," Edna said in astonishment.

"Now, let me show you some photos from my city.

She took an album with pictures from the shelf, showing her what was most beautiful, including the Champs Elysées, the Tuileries Garden, where locals went to relax, socialize, and entertain, Montmartre, the Louvre Museum, the garden and terraces of Versailles, the Arc of Triumph, the streets where people walked along the cafés with tables set outside, and many other photos showing the splendors of Paris.

Edna was amazed.

"I never could imagine that such beautiful places exist. Now, I have something delightful to think about."

"Let me tell you something, Edna. Read as much as possible and enrich your knowledge with history, geography, literature, art, and science. Education has no limits no matter in which part of the world you live. What you learn builds a world of yours that is more beautiful and richer than all the places that exist."

"I'll never forget what you said, Sister Catherine, and thank you for enlighten me. I don't want to impose, but may I ask your permission to come from time to time and have a talk with you?"

"I'll be very pleased to always talk with you, Edna, and you may come anytime you like."

From that day on, Edna went to Sister Catherine room as often as she could, and stayed there more than an hour, listening to stories that enriched her imagination. Sister Catherine showed her a lot of pictures in her albums, that each of them had a story to tell. Edna entered the world of beauty and magic that exists in reality.

The years passed and Edna finished her eight grade of school graduating with honors. Mrs.

Davis handed her the diploma congratulating her and wishing her much further success.

"If it's not hard for you, Mrs. Davis, could you make me a copy of my diploma?"

"With pleasure, Edna, and I would greatly like that you come from time to time and we could have a nice talk."

"With much gladness and thank you for everything."

Edna left her for the last time and returned to the convent. The superior mother asked her to see the diploma and said:

"It must be kept in your file next to your birth certificate. Now you will start preparing for the novitiate. Today you can have the day off and we'll start tomorrow."

Edna went to her room and was ready to carry out the plan she had thought of in detail: she was determined to leave the convent. For a start, she began to write an emotional letter to Sister Agnes, in which she mentioned her feelings and attachment to her. To Sister Catherine she thanked her for all the lessons she had received from her and for initiating her into the knowledge of a world, she did not know that existed. She thanked the superior mother for the years in which Her Reverence had given her shelter and food, mentioning that she could not become a nun because she had no vocation for such a purpose. Edna added in the letter that she borrowed a sum of money from the cash box and will return it as soon as she finds a job.

Next Saturday, Edna prepared her backpack with clothes, and took her last sketchbook. On Sunday morning, she told Sister Agnes that she was not feeling well, her stomach ached, she wanted to vomit, and she would not be able to attend the holy service.

"Stay in the room, and try to rest," Sister Agnes said.

"I'm very sorry".

Sister Agnes felt a slight tremor in Edna's voice, but at that moment, she thought that the girl was not feeling well and that's why her voice was shaking. She went to church with the other sisters and Edna stayed in her room.

Edna had two hours to finish what she had to do, until the nuns will return. She waited a while, and then placed the letters on the pillows of Sister Agnes and Sister Catherine. She went to the superior mother's office, put the letter on display on the desk, opened the cabinet, took the birth certificate from her file and replaced her school diploma with the copy; then she took a sum of money from the cash box, only that much as to be enough to pay the bus fare for a few days. She returned to her room, knelt down, and said a prayer, begging the Lord Creator to bless the choice she had made. Carefully, she put both documents and money in an inside pocket, took her backpack and a warm jacket, and left the room for the last time. Through the gate behind the building, Edna headed to the bus station. An hour later, she arrived in town.

Edna's disappearance caused a real storm at the convent. During the time of the service, Sister Agnes had a feeling of anxiety thinking about the trembling of the voice she had noticed when Edna talked to her; she was almost certain that it was not because Edna was not feeling well. She ran to her room and was convinced of her foreboding. She looked for her everywhere and was convinced that Edna was gone. When she found the letter, Sister Agnes burst into tears. Sister Catherine read Edna's letter and felt relief and gratitude in her soul. The superior mother had a furious reaction and called the sheriff on the phone, telling him to look for Edna and bring her to the convent. Mrs. Davis, who listened to the conversation, sincerely advised him:

"Don't look for her, George. Edna made the right decision. She is very intelligent; she is very talented; she is very beautiful; her place is not in the convent, but she is now free to follow her decision and make her life the way she wants."

"I think you're right, Magda."

A few days later, the sheriff told the superior mother that he had made every effort, but Edna had probably disappeared into a distant city.

Meanwhile, Edna had traveled from city to city only during the day; after three nights and four days she stopped when she ran out of money for the bus; she had only a little change left. All this time, she slept on benches, in parks, or in hidden places behind buildings; she only ate from the leftovers found in garbage cans of restaurants; she used public facilities to freshen up. The last destination was a very big city, with beautiful buildings, wide streets, and elegant shops. It was almost evening; Edna was tired, hungry, without any money, and starting to get discouraged. Walking slowly down the street, she stopped in front of a diner where a few customers sat at tables and finished their meals. She counted the small change she still had, and shyly went inside; she approached the counter, put all the change on top, and asked for a bagel and a glass of water. She took them and went to the window where the chairs were placed alongside a high table. When she had almost finished eating her bagel and was ready to leave, the woman at the counter approached her and asked:

"Do you know how to wash dishes?"

"Yes, I know."

"I can tell that you're a runaway. Don't be afraid; I know what you're going through. Come with me."

She took Edna to the kitchen where dishes and pots were everywhere. A man was cooking and arranging some meals on a plate. They both looked in their early fifties. The woman said:

"I'm Debra Williams, and this is my husband, Glen; we're the owners of this place. What is your name?"

"Edna Mathis."

"First, sit down Edna, and have a good meal. After that, you'll do the dishes."

Edna swallowed the food to the last crumb. She thanked the owners, asked for an apron and got to work. It was already closing time when she finished and the whole kitchen was spotless clean. The server, a young girl named Becky, had already gone home, and the owners were preparing to leave when Edna informed them that she had finished her work. They both inspected the kitchen and were very satisfied; all the pots, pans, and cutlery shone and were put in place. Mrs. Williams said:

"You did a very good work, Edna, and you have the job with a salary that pays for such work. We live upstairs above the diner, and up in the attic is a small room with a shower and toilet. You can live there. Tomorrow morning, we open the diner at eight o'clock, and you'll start working. Edna thanked them warmly, took her backpack, and went up to the attic where the room was very small, but very comfortable for her. She took a shower, went to bed, and slept for the first time lately, peacefully and without worries.

After one week, Edna got her first pay and she was very pleased thinking that now she earned the money for her work. One evening, before closing time, she addressed the couple:

"Mrs. and Mr. Williams, you have been awesomely good to me, you took me in without asking who I was and where I came from. I feel my duty that it's only fair to tell you the truth about me. She told them the entire story of her life in the convent.

"You had a hard time there, Edna and I barely can imagine how you survived", Mr. Williams said, and he asked:

"How much money do you owe them?"

Edna told them the exact amount she took from the cash box and said:

"As soon as I have enough I'll send everything back to them. Only, I don't know how the postal service works, so that they couldn't find my place of living from the address."

"No need, Edna", Mr. Williams said. "We'll send them the money, and you can keep everything you work for. And…Edna, let's call each other by first name."

Edna had tears in her eyes and found no words to thank them, but they understood her feelings, and were happy to help her.

The diner opened at eight in the morning, and closed between three and five in the afternoon, when Edna had to do her work in the kitchen. The closing time was nine in the evening and Edna had to work after, for about two hours. Usually when customers were coming, she had little to do in the kitchen and could spend some free time in her room, or outside. She drew the portraits of both Debra and Glen, and gave them as a reminder of her. They were very pleased, congratulated her on her talent, and hung them on the wall of the diner so that customers could see them. Edna liked to take a walk and watch the people passing by, or window shopping, looking at the expensive clothes and art objects displayed in the boutiques windows. One block away from the diner, she saw a high school and entered inside, to ask about night classes. The person in charge gave her all the information saying that if she was interested she could enroll in fall and the program was between five and nine o'clock. Edna had something to think about, but her mind was already working a plan.

She talked to Mrs. and Mr. Williams who had no objection as long as Edna could do her work in the diner. She said that she could manage very well, both.

In fall, Edna enrolled in high school and made a very detailed schedule to do her work in the kitchen and attend the night classes. She did her job as before, and woke up at five in the morning, doing her school homework. She learned quickly in school how to work with computers, bought a laptop and her homework became much easier. Not one day she missed her job or a class.

Edna graduated at the age of seventeen and she got the diploma of high school that she badly wanted. She continued to wash dishes and clean the kitchen like before, but her mind was eager to go farther. She now had more time to make a plan for the future; her desire was to go to college and pursue a career. She wanted to study art and continue working in a painting workshop or museum, or to be a teacher. There were many possibilities that opened up in front of her and it was up to her to decide how to move on, but first, she had to get an education in college. Edna remembered the words of Sister Catherine: *Education has no limits no matter in which part of the world you live. What you learn builds a world of yours that is more beautiful and richer than all the places that exist.* For this, first of all, she needed a more consistent material support and a job that would allow her to work regular hours in such a way that she could have enough time left for learning. She thought it would be a good job to work in an office as a clerk or secretary and could then enroll in college for evening classes. However, all the jobs listed in the newspapers that would have suited her, required experience. Edna was saddened to think that her chances of going to college were slim, almost none.

With a troubled mind, one Sunday afternoon, she took the bus without any special aim, and arrived in the neighborhood of the rich and famous where everything had an exorbitant price. Edna got off the bus and started walking the wide streets looking at the sumptuous houses with gardens and pools, thinking that those people had no problems that could not be solved. She reached a large glass-walled building and approached. Inside she saw elegantly dressed people moving from place to place in a large room where the walls were covered with photographs. Without thinking that she was not dressed at the level of those inside, Edna entered the room and began to look at the exposed photos. Most were black and white and showed various subjects with buildings, bridges, streets, and people. Edna came closer and began to study carefully the details that she found very interesting. Some had attracted her attention more; they were very well executed portraits of very beautiful women and young men. She paused in front of them for a long time, following the outlines of the features, and the blend between shadow and light, which was amazing. Edna was so focused on analyzing the photos that she forgot about her problems and lost track of the time when she realized it was late in the evening, and she had to leave. As she headed to the door, she heard a voice behind her:

"May I take a picture of you?"

He was a rather young man, good looking, who carried a complicated camera.

"Can I stop you?", Edna asked.

"You can, but why? My name is Paul Clarke, I took all these photos, and I own this gallery. You have an unusual beauty and I would appreciate very much your kindness to allow me to exhibit your picture in my gallery."

"I'm not properly dressed for a picture, especially for your gallery."

"I'm not interested in your outfit; only in your face. What is your name?"

"Edna Mathis."

"Would you smile for me, Edna, and allow me to take your picture?"

"Don't you ever give up?"

"No. Please smile."

His persistence made her smile and he took several pictures of her from different angles. She was stunningly beautiful when she smiled.

"You'll get paid for these pictures, Edna. Tell me your address and I'll send you the money. Or rather, if you prefer, you can come to my studio, which is around the corner, we'll make some more pictures, and you'll be highly paid. Here is my card. What do you say?"

"Nothing for now. I have to talk to my mother first. She is very strict."

"I can see that you're scared and I understand. I'll tell you what: if you decide to come, you may ask your mother to accompany you as a chaperon. Then you'll feel confident and safe. What do you say?"

"I'll talk to her."

"If you decide to come, the best time will be Wednesday afternoon, after five."

Edna left with many new thoughts in her mind. She arrived home almost at closing time, and she had to start her job in the kitchen. Debra and Glen were waiting for her to come from town, and could close the diner. She told them the whole story and asked their opinion.

"I think this might be dangerous for you", Glen said.

"I think this is a big opportunity for you to have a more fulfilling life, maybe even a career", Debra said. "As much as I like you to stay with us forever, I know that one day will come when you'll have to leave and have a better life. I'll tell you what: I'll go with you and then I'll be able to make my mind better. What do you say?"

"I like that, Debra, and if you come with me, I'll feel safe."

"I think that you should go with Edna. I feel more comfortable if she will not be alone. I'll manage to take care of the customers with Becky, don't worry about", Glen said.

Wednesday, before five o'clock, they took the car and Debra drove to the address. The studio was very big; everywhere, lamps, screens, and cameras of all sizes showed that it was a rich and busy place. Next to the far sidewall were a podium and some chairs. Paul greeted them at the door:

"I'm glad you could come, Edna."

She made the presentations:

"This is my mother, Debra Williams, and this is Paul Clarke."

"Pleased to meet you", they both said.

"Have a seat, and I'll show you the pictures I've made. He took from his desk a big envelope with Edna's photos. They were stunning. She looked like a professional model.

"I don't know what to say, Paul, except that I barely can recognize myself."

"Don't try to be modest. You should be proud of your beauty."

"These pictures are above my admiration, Mr. Clarke."

"Thank you Mrs. Williams. I'm a professional photographer and I choose very carefully my subjects, the places and people who are of interest to me. These photos will be displayed in my gallery and I'll be honored if you come over to look at them, after two weeks. Now, let's start a little session and see how Edna can move on that podium. First, my assistant will give her some help with a dress and some advices."

A young girl showed up and took Edna to a next room. After a little while, they both came back. Edna was dressed in a long pale lavender thick veil gown, had a white transparent veil scarf around her neck, and wore gold sandals with high heels. Her body was statuary, and the clothing highlighted the splendor of her shapes and delicate lines. Both Debra and Paul were stunned when they saw her and could not utter a word. She was like a beauty more imaginary than real. Edna smiled when she saw their amazement and bowed gracefully to them. Paul recovered first from his astonishment and without another word invited her to step up on the podium. Helped by the assistant who changed the cameras, he began to take pictures one after the other, telling Edna how to behave and following her every move. After about an hour, Edna got tired and asked to finish the session. The assistant took the cameras and accompanied Edna to the other room to change.

"These pictures will be on display in the gallery a month from now. I will send you an invitation when the exhibition opens."

Paul was still in an atmosphere of astonishment, as he had become taciturn and looked preoccupied. He went to his desk, opened a notebook, wrote something, and handed a check for payment to Edna. When both Edna and Debra saw the amount, they were ready to faint.

That same evening, Edna addressed the Williams couple:

"You are like my parents that I never had. You saved my life and I will always be grateful for everything you have done for me. But now, it's time to move on and make a career. I want to enroll in college and achieve what I want to continue working on. I will stay with you until you find someone to replace me. I hope you understand me. Glen replied with emotion in his voice:

"Edna, you have been a great joy to us and we understand exactly that the time has come to move forward with your life."

"You are an honest, hardworking, considerate girl, and it was a great joy to have you with us," Debra added. "You will always be dear to us and we will remember you with longing and pleasure. It is very good that you have decided to study in college and make a career in your life. There is no need to wait until we find someone to replace you. We wish you all the best in the world and to succeed in achieving everything you set out to do."

"Thank you very much. I will come from time to time to visit you and keep you up to date with everything that is happening in my life."

They hugged warmly and with tears in their eyes.

The next day Edna opened a bank account and deposited the entire amount she had received from Paul. She found a small one bedroom apartment at second floor in a building on a quiet street, that she rented and furnished with everything she needed. It was about a half hour by bus far from college. In the following days, she began to visit the college library and find out exactly what courses she needed to take. After deciding to take art and literature courses, she went to college and enrolled for the first year, which was about to begin in a month. She had enough time until then to take driving lessons and she got her license. With help from Glen, she chose a small car; put down payment and everything became much easier for her.

Edna sent a thankful card to Paul, giving her address and phone number asking to send her the invitation to the opening, and mentioning that she was looking forward to seeing the photos. Two days later, when she returned from the library in the evening, she found in front of the door a huge basket of flowers with a card from Paul. She entered inside, placed the flowers on the table, and prepared to eat something when someone rang the doorbell. It was Paul.

"May I come in?"

"Can I stop you?"

"No."

"Then you have to come in. Thank you very much for the flowers."

Paul came inside and out of a big envelope took her photos and lined them up on the table. Edna covered her mouth with both hands when she saw them and could not utter a word.

"I thought so," Paul said.

Edna calmed down from her surprise and managed to speak:

"I would never have imagined that I would see something like these. They are wonderful Paul. I can't believe it's me in these photos."

"You are beautiful, but I have talent! Is there anything to eat in this house? I'm hungry."

"A sandwich with a glass of milk."

Edna set the table for both and they had a pleasant conversation while they ate. It was late and Edna waited for him to leave.

"May I stay?"

"Can I stop you?"

"Yes, you can."

In that night, Edna grew more mature by learning what men always expected, and found out that they never behave just as friends, only.

One evening, Edna asked Paul to pose for her to draw his portrait. Only out of curiosity did Paul accept. After almost an hour, when he saw it, he said:

"You caught even the finest lines on my face. I didn't know you had such a talent."

"You didn't know anything about me, so don't be surprised."

"Sign it."

"Why?"

"If you ever become famous, this portrait will be worth a lot and I'll be rich."

They both had a big laugh.

The opening of the gallery with the exhibition of Edna's photos was a huge success. The spectators crowded in front of her pictures, expressing their admiration and congratulating Paul for his wonderful work. Debra and Glen had also come and praised Edna for her accomplishment wishing her all the best in her future.

Not long after, a fashion magazine bought some of the photos and displayed one of them on the cover. Edna had a great pleasure, but did not rely too much on her success because it was not part of her plans for the future.

College classes had begun, and Edna was diligently focusing on her learning. She liked the courses she had chosen, the teachers, and her colleagues. A lot of time, she spent in the library, learning and reading additional specialized books in order to enrich her knowledge as much as possible. Sometimes Edna thought of Paul and analyzed her feelings for him. Apart from the admiration she had for his talent and work, she had no other. They had nothing in common to make her approach him more, and establish a closer connection. They were very different from each other and their relationship had slowly cooled without regrets on both sides.

Sometimes, on Sunday morning, Edna went to church, sat on the bench and listened to the holy service she knew so well. Many memories came to her mind, some of them very dear, which she always will treasure. After church, she went to see Debra and Glen, telling them everything that happened to her lately. They always had advices to give, and she was glad to take them.

Time passed by, Edna graduated from college and starting looking for a job. She had several propositions but none of them seemed appealing.

One day she received a phone call from a man by his name Richard Werner, saying that he was the representative of a fashion agency and wanted to have an interview with her; he said that she was highly recommended by Paul Clarke who worked for him as a photographer. Edna accepted, and on that day at the appointed time, she showed up at the address given to her. It was a sumptuous building with luxurious halls, lit from all angles and the floor was covered with expensive rugs from one wall to another. Edna took the elevator and on the sixth floor, she arrived in a huge room with all sorts of arrangements, lamps, runways, stages, garment racks, and rows of chairs. Busy people moved everywhere, carrying something in their hands or hanging from their shoulders. She was expected, and an assistant led her to Richard Werner's office, who was sitting at a desk with some papers in front of him. He was a handsome, tall man, with an athletic body, dark golden hair, hazel eyes, looked very distinguished, and must have been about thirty years of age or even younger. He got up and invited her to sit in one of the armchairs. Edna waited for the conversation to begin, but he kept staring at her. Paul had not exaggerated when he described her beauty; it was truly remarkable. After a few minutes, he asked her what experience she had in modeling.

"None."

"Would you like to represent as an agency's model the most recent fashion line?"

"I have no idea what you're talking about. I just finished college and I'm looking for a job. If you have something right for me, I would gladly accept."

"Get up and walk around the room."

Edna looked at him in astonishment and did as she was told.

"Admirably!" he exclaimed.

"For the beginning, I offer you to appear at the next exhibition, displaying the fashion dresses that have been executed recently. Until the opening, you will learn how to move, how to gesture, how to walk on the runway and all that is required of a model. What do you think?"

"I can try."

"Very good. The first lesson will be tomorrow at ten o'clock in the morning. Be punctual and without any fear. I predict a great success."

Edna quickly learned everything a model needed to know. Together with five other models, they did daily rehearsals until the opening, which proved to be an unexpected success. Spectators seated on chairs on either side of the runway looked at each model walking back and forth, and at the dresses, they presented, taking notes and photos. The fashion line in that day, demonstrated a resounding success, bringing a lot of income to the agency, and the models were paid generously. Edna was invited several more times to present the same fashion line in front of potential buyers who had all the resources to win in competitions. She was paid more than she had ever expected, and with the money she had before, she was provided for all her needs quite a long enough time. First thing she did was to buy a dishwasher machine and sent it to Debra and Glen. They both cried of so much joy, and then let go the girl who did the job. After that, Edna decided to send a sum of money to Mother Superior to help the convent and to Mrs. Davis to help the village school. She appealed to Glen for this favor, emphasizing that no name of the sender should be mentioned and that the sending of the money should remained anonymous. Ever since, she sent money regularly, to both.

However, it was time for her to give up modeling and to pursue her career. Edna bit farewell from Richard Werner, thanking him for the opportunity given to her to work as a model in his agency.

"May I see you again?, he asked.

"Certainly. You have my phone number and it will be a pleasure for me to meet you any time, at your convenience."

"Don't be surprised if I call you one day."

They shook hands, and Edna left.

Chapter 2

Later on

In college, Edna took a photography course and proved that she knew how to handle the camera very well, while in terms of subjects, her artistic talent was an undeniable factor. She intended to take artistic photographs, which she would later exhibit in a gallery. For that, however, she needed development equipment and a darkroom. In order to have all the working conditions, it was necessary for her to move to a two-bedroom apartment, one of which she turned it into a darkroom. The apartment was in the same building on the third floor, so it was easy to move her belongings one level up. A beautiful spring with clear days and abundant vegetation bloomed in parks and gardens. People were walking the streets; children were playing in the backyards of the houses; Edna had multiple choices for the topics that interested her. Apart from the rich nature, she liked to photograph people's faces, first asking their permission and if they agreed, they smiled with pleasure. She was especially attracted to the faces of elderly people, who expressed sadness and suffering that could be read in their eyes and on their accentuated wrinkles. Arriving home, Edna developed the films until late in the evening, and the photos taken in that day gave her great satisfaction. Sometimes she chose subjects she liked best, and painted them on canvas in oil or watercolor. Mostly, she liked to paint faces from her photographs, and she spent a lot of time in doing the details, accentuating on the shades of light and dark. In few weeks, she had enough photos and paintings to display in a gallery.

One day, she received a phone call from Richard expressing his desire to see her. Edna was very pleased and invited him for the next day. He came in the afternoon with a bouquet of blue lilac and a large box elegantly tied with a white bow. Edna invited him inside, and was very surprised when she opened the box. It was the dress and cape she had wore at the opening of the fashion line with which she had a huge success.

"I was very pleased to show off their elegance then, and thank you very much, but where can I wear this outfit now? I don't see any particular occasion of wearing it again."

"We'll find an opportunity sooner or later. I'm sure you'll be the center of attraction as you were then. Now, tell me how do you spend your time. What did you do lately?"

"I worked a lot. Come, I'll show you."

In front of his astonished eyes, she displayed the photos and paintings she did. He took a careful look at each and whispered:

"I don't know what to say except that they are marvelous. You have an exceptional talent especially for details. What do you intend to do with your collection?"

"I'm looking forward to find a small gallery and exhibit them. Maybe, even I could sell a few. First, I need to find a location, and then do some advertising in papers."

"I can help with my experience. Let's find a place and I'll do the advertising. Then we'll hang them on the walls and open it for the public. I foresee a big success."

"I don't know how to thank you, Richard. I can use much of your help, since I don't have any experience in this field of commercializing my work."

"All must be framed. I will bring the frames for your photos and paintings. There is no need for expensive frames, but simple ones, because connoisseurs are only interested in the value of the work and not in the frames. I'll look for a location and I'll call you. Now, I have to leave. It is a great pleasure seeing you again."

He left, and Edna thought that maybe not all men are alike. Richard was warm and caring; he appreciated sincerely her work, and offered to help without her asking for it. She liked his behavior, his smooth voice, his attitude, his hazel eyes changing color from green to light brown to gold; very much, she liked his smile. In that night, she slept with sweet dreams.

Richard found a location not far from his agency. It was a small building but very suitable for the exhibition that Edna wanted to do. He told her on the phone and went to pick her up from home.

Edna was delighted with the choice Richard had made for her; she began to measure the length of the walls and the possible distances between the exhibits.

"This is wonderful, Richard! This is exactly what I need!"

"I'm glad you like it. Now, I have to ask you something."

"Say it."

"I would like us to go some place and talk. Let's go to the park and have a seat by the lake. What do you think?"

"Let's go, then."

They reached the shore of the lake, and sat on a bench watching the waves rippled by a light breeze.

"Edna, I am very attracted to your personality and I suspect that you also enjoy being in my company. However, we do not know each other and we know almost nothing about each other. I want to be honest with you and tell you about my life, who I am, what my ambitions were, and where am I going. I think that's right on my part and it's a duty I owe you. I hope you understand."

"I understand, Richard. I feel the same desire to tell you about my life and me. I wanted to propose this conversation, but you decided before me. It means that it is a beginning of good understanding between us, no matter what the consequences of this discussion will be."

"Very well then. My life has not been spectacular, but quite acceptable. My mother, Estelle, was French by origin, and she was a music teacher; my father Aden, was German by origin and he was a surgeon. I'm fluent in both languages, and at fifteen, I studied piano at the conservatory. My parents came to this country before I was born, and died in a plane crash when I was twenty; I had to work and learn at the same time, wanting more than anything to have an education. I studied fine arts and philosophy, gained a lot of knowledge, and had a strong desire to achieve something useful in life. I didn't even know what to start with and I didn't have the material means to pursue a career to my liking. One day, a very good friend of mine invited me to go with him at a party given by a very rich and powerful woman by her name Mona Cox who sponsored the most famous fashion designers. He suggested to rent a tuxedo and not to look like a bumb. That evening I saw for the first time how very rich people live. The mansion I entered was of a remarkable luxury, with marble floors, expensive carpets, and original paintings. The host was very kind, received us with friendship, smiling and introducing us to the other guests who were probably from the same social class. Mona Cox was very elegant, talked a lot with each guest, and went from one to another being sure that everyone was comfortable. She asked me some personal questions to which I answered hesitantly, then she inquired what school I have and if I work somewhere. I told her the truth, she looked at me for few minutes, then she said that she would have something that might interest me; it was a position in one of her agencies, where I could promote models for fashion lines. I knew nothing about models, but the next week, I started my job and it turned out that I could manage it very well. Soon, Mona offered me a partnership in her business, and gave me an income beyond my expectations. However, her intentions turned out to be completely different from benefaction. She asked me to move in with her, saying that I could have a part of the mansion and that step would be in favor of the business reputation. I did something naïve and I accepted, because after a short time she asked me to marry her. She assured me that it would only be a marriage of convenience, just to attract the rich and famous people, because my name along with hers would bring immense profits and fame. For the second time I made a big mistake. Mona was much older than me and soon revealed her true character; she became jealous, possessive, authoritarian, controlling all my actions and behaviors. It had become impossible for me to endure and I filed for divorce. She told me that she loved me and would never divorce me, because I belonged only to her. I announced then that I would move out of her house and we would break up. She made a terrible scene, but I took my things and left. We haven't seen each other since, but my countless requests for divorce through a lawyer were rejected on the grounds that I owed her an amount of money that was actually ridiculous, exceeded all the income of her business, and of course, I had no way to pay it. My only hope is that one day, Mona will get bored or she will find another companion, and I will have peace. For now we are separated, and the situation for me is unclear and uncertain."

Richard made a long pause, then looked deep in Edna's eyes and asked:

"Can you accept me the way I am?"

"I'll accept you any way you are."

He took her in his arms and whispered:

"I worked a lot with models but only saw their beautiful faces and the way they moved around. I never new anything about their mind or their soul.

Since I've met you, for the first time I could connect to the beauty of your mind, could feel the deepness of your soul, and I fell in love with you."

"I love you, Richard."

They kissed and looked into each other's eyes, understanding the deepness of their love.

"Now, it's your turn. Would you like to tell me something about your life?"

She told him everything to the smallest details. He was very impressed, the same as she was after he told her the story of his life. He took her in his arms and kissed her with all the warmth of his heart. A strong bond started growing between them, not ever to be broken.

Edna told Debra and Glen about Richard and how much they love each other. They both were happy for her and asked when they can meet him.

"In a couple of weeks the gallery will be ready and you'll both come to the opening. He will be there."

Edna asked Richard to pose for her to paint his portrait. He was enthusiastic when it was ready:

"Looks even better than me! Are you going to exhibit it in the gallery?"

"No, and it's not for sale. I put my love for you in every single brushstroke and in every drop of paint. I want to keep it here to look at it and to have you all the time with me."

"I'm falling in love with you over and over, again and again."

"I know."

For almost two weeks, they both worked hard to make the most attractive exhibit of Edna's photographs and paintings. The gallery opened on a Sunday, and people started to come in, alone or in a group. Debra and Glen closed the diner for that day and showed up early, to be among the first ones to see Edna's work.

It seemed that the public was interested in the exhibition; some spectators watched the paintings and photos closely, talking to each other, others watched them from a distance, sitting on the benches in the middle of the room. Edna was excited and Richard was trying to calm her down:

"Everything will be fine, as I predicted. I want to meet your adoptive parents."

Edna took his hand and approached Debra and Glen. From the beginning, they liked each other and began to address by their first names.

"Our daughter has a remarkable talent, don't you think, Richard?" Glen said.

"She is not only very talented but she is an extraordinary person from all points of view. People like her are very rare in today's world."

"You two are very close, as I saw, and that makes me very happy, because finally, Edna has someone to share her life, with all the joys and sorrows that come on the way," Debra added.

"Yes, Debra, Edna and I, we have a special harmony and many common affinities that we share between us with all the sincerity and love we have for each other."

Edna sold ten photos and four paintings, all very well paid. The next day, an article praising her work with a very appreciative critique appeared in a local art magazine.

"Didn't I tell you so?", Richard asked.

"Yes, you did, but I was scared to raise my expectations too high."

"Now you can, and you should. Where would you like us to go celebrate your success?"

"We know each other for some time and I don't even know where you live. I would like very much to see your place."

"I never asked you to come to my place just because I didn't want you to be disappointed. You see, I make good money and still I live in a modest apartment where no one comes to visit me and where I'm alone with only my thoughts. However, since you asked me, let's go to my place and have a celebration."

They stopped on the way and Richard bought some food and drinks. Once inside, Edna was pleased with the neatness of his apartment, but somehow she was surprised:

"I was expecting you to have a piano, since you told me that you went to the conservatory."

"My mother was my teacher and she encouraged me to love and study music. I even played a solo piano concert with the local orchestra, when I was seventeen years old. My mother was so proud of me that made me cry. Ever since she died, I didn't touch the piano."

"I understand your pain, and I'm here for you now, and forever, if you let me."

"Don't ever leave me, Edna."

"Be sure of that."

On his desk, she saw the pictures of his parents, who both were smiling and very good looking. Next to them, was her photo taken by the time when they met at the fashion line opening.

"I wanted you to be with me ever since we've met. I wish I could have your portrait, but I can't paint."

"I'll make one for you. I experienced a lot drawing myself, looking in the mirror when I was in the convent. I told you about my sketches from that time."

"Yes, you told me, and I can't wait to have your portrait. Now, let's have something to eat, because I'm hungry."

They had a great time, and knowing that nothing could ever take them apart.

In the days that followed, Richard had a new feeling rising in his soul. It was as if his mother was next to him and encouraged him to come even closer to Edna. Then an idea came to him that had not crossed his mind. He appeared at her door smiling and said:

"Know something? This Sunday we go to the concert hall to listen to classical music. The show will start with Franz Schubert's *Unfinished Symphony*, and then a young Chinese soloist will perform Edvard Grieg's *Piano Concerto*. What do you think?"

"I don't know anything about music, especially classical."

"It's time to introduce you, and I'm sure it will conquer you. I have already taken the tickets for a loge to have the best audition and view. I suggest you wear the outfit that I brought you and that you wore at the opening of the fashion line; I'll wear a tuxedo. I'm convinced that you'll capture the attention of everyone in the hall."

On Sunday evening, they went to the concert and sat in the front row of the loge. The elegant people were preparing to take their places and the orchestrators on stage were checking their instruments. Edna had never seen anything like it before, but she controlled her curiosity so as not to attract attention. Some people kept starring at her, whispering among each other, while she was admiring the paintings of the ceiling and the luxury of that place. When the conductor appeared, there was complete silence, and the concert began with the Schubert's *Symphony*. Indeed, Edna was impressed by the harmony of the music and the cohesive whole of the instruments. At the end, the applause was huge, and the conductor had to appear several times and bow to the audience.

"Did you like it?" Richard asked.

"Very much. I've never heard anything so beautiful. Actually, I never knew that something so beautiful existed. You have to forgive my ignorance."

"It's not your fault. You had a hard life, my love."

After a few minutes, the soloist appeared, followed by the conductor, both of whom were received with applause. Under the baton of the conductor, the soloist began the first notes accompanied by the orchestra, then revealed his talent in full force. Edna's attention at the same time was drawn to Richard's face that seemed transposed into another world. Tears had begun to flow without him trying to wipe them away. Edna took his hand and felt him tremble. All the emotions of his past hidden for so long, appeared on the surface and he could not retain them. He felt Edna's hand and recovered in time so that he didn't burst into tears. Somehow, he managed to control himself, caressed the hand that protected him, and smiled calmly.

After the last note, the audience exploded into applause that seemed endless, while the soloist and conductor shook hands and bowed to the audience. They were called to the stage several times, until the applause was over and people were getting ready to leave.

"Did you like it?" Richard asked.

"I can't wake up from amazement and admiration. It was something beautiful that I never knew existed."

"The symphony and the piano concert were very well performed. The pianist is very young but shows a lot of talent. I liked the concert and I'm glad I came."

On the way out he asked:

"Are we going to your place or mine?"

"Yours. You have to reconcile with your past memories, and I won't let you cry alone."

"You never cease to amaze me."

"I'm happy that I can amaze you."

It was late night when they arrived home. First thing, Richard did, was to give a long look to the picture of his mother, and whispered:

"Thank you Mom", but he didn't cry.

He took Edna in his arms, kissed her with passion and said:

"Thank you, my love, for being with me. I'm free now of my repressed memories. Next Sunday we'll go the Opera House."

"I don't know anything about opera."

"I don't know much either, but I like to listen to the music and especially to the voices. Almost all lyrics are based on tragic stories, and that's why the music is dramatic and emotional. Maybe this time you'll cry and I'll hold your hand."

"You wish. Now it's past midnight and let's have some sleep. Tomorrow we both have work to do."

Edna's gallery had to be completed with new photos and paintings, so that it could be opened for the next exhibition. She walked the streets and parks again, photographing faces, groups of people and landscapes, which she developed for hours, then comparing their artistic quality and choosing the most successful ones for the gallery. She then made paintings inspired by the most interesting photographs, and compared them by finding the right place next to each other, examining the subjects and the details of the colors. Richard's opinions mattered a lot to Edna. He also examined everything she did and expressed his choices for the gallery, which rarely were different from hers. She asked him:

"Do you love your job at the agency?"

"I hate it. I studied art and always wanted to work in my field, but never had the chance. I wanted to teach art or be a museum curator, to develop my knowledge, but never had time to look for a position, and I have to live with what I have."

"Maybe, one day, your wish we'll be fulfilled."

The following Sunday they went to the Opera House where the show was Giacomo Puccini's *La Bohème*. Richard told Edna the storyline that impressed her and she became very curious how it would combine with the music. The Opera House was even more elegant than the Concert Hall, which proved to Edna that it was a place, which exhibited big luxury and wealth. They took their seats in the loge, which was close to the stage, and the opera begun with the motif of the bohemians, without overture, as typical of Puccini. Edna was conquered from the first scene by the melodic music and the voices of the performers. From time to time Richard looked at her and smiled at the concentration and emotion shown on her face. The scene from the last act in which Mimi was on her deathbed impressed Edna more with the beautiful music than with the action and the actors' stage play. She started crying, and Richard held her hand while she discretely tried to wipe away her tears.

From then on, they went often to watch an opera show or a concert. Richard proved to be a great teacher in Edna's musical education, while she became a very diligent pupil.

The gallery was a great success, and Edna received very encouraging and appreciative reviews in local art magazines; her name, although at the beginning of her career, had already begun to be recognized as very promising in the artistic community. Some of her work was sold with well-paid prices and Edna made quite a lot of money. She was at the height of her happiness together with Richard, who gave her all his moral support and showed his love for her at every step on the way. The next move Edna was thinking about was to open a studio and teach painting and photography lessons in addition to maintaining the gallery. Richard along with Debra and Glen enthusiastically approved of her plans.

Next evening, she started cooking dinner, while many thoughts circled in her mind. She decided to tell him the deepest of her secrets. He came home, kissed her, freshened up, and said that he was hungry. Edna put her arms around his neck, looked him deep into his eyes, and whispered:

"I'm pregnant."

He rolled his eyes in wonder, and opened his mouth to speak, but could not make a sound. Finally, he gathered his senses and managed to ask:

"This means that we are going to have a baby?"

"According to the natural laws, this is exactly what it means."

"We are going to have a real baby?"

"Most certainly, not a synthetic one."

"Then you're not supposed to work anymore, especially carrying those heavy cameras and photographing the world. You have to stay inside and I'll do the entire house work. You have to be careful at each step you make, so that you not fall down."

"Anything else you recommend? If you have more to say, this is your last chance to advise me."

"There is more to say but I don't have in mind something specific now."

"Good! I'll tell you then: I read all the books and I know exactly what to do. I have to work, to go out and shop, to enjoy what I like, and especially not let you step on my nerves with your constant worries! Now, do we understand each other?"

"I just want to take care of you and the baby, the best way I can."

"The best way is the one I just told you. If you'll be around all the time, I'll start screaming so loud that the entire neighborhood will hear me. We both have to follow our daily schedule as usually, and then we'll understand each other perfectly."

"I love you like nobody can love you, and now I love our baby too."

"Oh, what am I going to do with you? I love you the same, and having our baby is the biggest happiness I could ever hope for."

He took her in his arms and kissed her with all the warmth of his heart.

One morning, while working on the easel, someone rang the doorbell and Edna went to see who might have been at that hour. She opened the door and there, was a corpulent woman, elegantly dressed, in her early fifties probably.

"I'm Mona Cox, Richard's wife, and I want to have a few words with you."

Edna invited her inside but she refused to sit down.

"I will be very brief in what I have to say. Richard is my husband and although we are separated, I want him back because I love him and he belongs to me. You are an obstacle to his return home; I give you advice for your own good, to let him go and leave him alone."

"Is this a threat?"

"It is simply an advice for now. Listen to it and follow it so as not to cause unpleasant consequences. I hope you understood the reason for this meeting. Good day, Miss Mathis."

Edna was left with a great trouble in her soul and many upsetting thoughts began to appear in her mind. Indeed, that woman had threatened her and proved to be very dangerous. Edna thought not to tell Richard about her visit, as it could provoke a scene of anger against Mona, which would have made the whole situation even worse. She couldn't tell Debra and Glen either, because they would both become extremely worried, and that wouldn't help clarify the situation. Edna decided to keep the story of that day to herself for a while, and see what will happen next. Measures to prevent serious consequences she could not foresee at all, except the execution of the advice to let Richard go, which Edna was not at all inclined to do.

That evening Richard came earlier from the agency and Edna was preparing dinner without any enthusiasm.

"You are very quiet. Did something unpleasant happen? ", he asked.

"No, my dear, I'm probably a little tired after all the hustle and bustle of opening the gallery. Don't worry, it will pass."

"I have an idea that might help. It's almost Christmas time; let's go to a mountain resort for a short vacation of a few days and have our first Christmas holiday together, just the two of us. It would do us good, we could rest, and we could have a wonderful time taking small walks and visiting the surroundings. What do you think?"

"I think it's a great idea and it would really suit both of us."

"Let's see which places are more likable."

Edna brought an atlas with extensive descriptions and they both chose a mountain resort that they found more attractive. Richard made reservation at the best hotel, and after a couple of days, they packed some belongings, took winter clothing, and left in the morning.

The road to the mountains was crowded with tourists, especially skiers, but they arrived safely after almost two hours. The city was very small, and adorned with lights that lined the trees and all the cottages, giving the impression of a real holiday. The room was spacious overlooking the slope, and very comfortable. Both were in a wonderful mood and glad that they decided to have a few days of vacation in which to be away from any problems.

They unpacked their luggage, and went for a short walk on the crowded streets with tourists rushing to the ski slope. Richard made a proposal:

"We can rent equipment and go try the slope."

"How do we get up there? By car, by plane, or by train? "

"With the ski lift"

"Not in your dreams. I don't know how to ski, I don't know how to skate, and I don't know how to swim; and about that cart hanging from wires, having a precipice underneath, I don't get on it. I only know how to walk on solid ground that is under my feet, and gives me security. If you have fun, rent equipment and try your sports talents, while I'm here and I'm waiting for you to come back in one piece ".

"I have no idea how to ski, and if you want to know, same as you, I feel safer when I stroll and take a pleasant walk. We are from the same tribe, with the same character traits. "

"Which is?"

"The tribe of thinkers."

"Maybe you're right. However, you have an athletic body; how did you get it?

"When I was young I used to do workout a lot in a gym and make sure that I keep my body in good shape. What about you? How did you get such a beautiful body?"

"My mother made me like that. I'm thinking often about her, how she was, how she looked, and what she thought about me when I was born. She never looked for me, trying to find out what happened to me. Sometimes I love her, and sometimes I hate her. I never knew what the love of a mother was, and I always missed that."

"No matter how she was, you became a wonderful person, not only looking awesomely beautiful, but exceptionally talented and intelligent, hard working, honest, considerate, and caring for everyone around you. You made alone your wonderful personality, without any help from other people. Your mother would be very proud of you and I'm sure, if she would know, she would have no regrets for giving you birth. I'm sure she is thinking of you with love, every passing day in her life."

"Maybe, so. You always find the right words to make me feel good. I love you dearly."

"You are my life and I cannot even imagine how I could live without you."

In the middle of the crowded street, they embraced each other and kissed with all the love they felt for each other.

It started to snow and it was time to return to the hotel. They had lunch in the dining room, which was beautifully decorated, and very elegant, and then went to the room for a short rest. It was almost evening, the tourists were returning from skiing, and the hall was full of noise and good cheer. The next day after a nutritious breakfast, they went to visit the souvenir boutiques. They bought something for Debra and Glen, deciding to celebrate the New Year together at a restaurant with music and dance. In a boutique, Edna saw two figurines that had caught her eye. They were about four inches tall, carved in jade, and represented a boy and a girl, smiling. Edna analyzed them carefully and liked them very much. In college, she knew how to check gemstones for real or fake. She held by turn, each figurine in her hand and felt its temperature. It warmed up at her touch and then she set it aside; it cooled down very quickly, meaning that they were made of real jade.

"The girl is Edna and she is yours, and the boy is Richard and he is mine. Now, you pay because they are very expensive."

"I'll keep the figurine with me, as a dear reminder of these moments."

"Me too."

On Christmas Eve, the hotel manager had decorated the dining room with flowers and lights and for each guest there was a small gift placed on the plate. A small orchestra on stage invited the guests to dance. Edna and Richard stepped on the floor and enjoyed the melodious songs, having a wonderful time, and dancing till late night.

Next morning, they went home, taking with them dear memories, to be always cherished and never to be forgotten.

The New Year's Eve was spent as they planned. Together with Debra and Glen, they went to a luxurious restaurant with music, dance, and good food. They had a tremendous time, joking, laughing, having interesting conversation, and dancing all night. Debra and Glen behaved like teenagers, and she said:

"I've never had such a good time since we've been married, and that was thirty years ago."

"We have good time everyday working in the diner", Glen said, laughing.

"Not exactly like tonight, but I love being with you all the time."

It was almost morning when they all went home, and had a restful and well-deserved sleep. After two days, Edna and Richard started working with fresh enthusiasm.

One afternoon close to dusk, Edna went to the store to do some shopping. When she was ready to enter the car, she was attacked from behind, knocked on the ground, punched, and kicked until she lost consciousness. A man in the car next to hers saw the whole scene but did not intervene; he immediately called the police and the paramedic, then started the car and disappeared. Help came quickly; the police looked for witnesses but no one could say what happened. Edna was immediately taken to the emergency room and doctors began to consult her. In her wallet was Richard's phone, who was called urgently and came in a few minutes.

He trembled when he asked what had happened and the nurse told him that Edna was unconscious and the doctors were examining her. Richard immediately called Debra and Glen, they came over and were just as scared as he was. An hour later, the doctor appeared and told them that Edna had been brutally beaten, had two broken ribs, a dislocated shoulder, and her body was full of bruises; she has deep cuts in her upper leg, and lost a lot of blood. He also said that Edna was pregnant and probably by instinct she rolled on her belly protecting the baby, because her pregnancy was not affected. The doctor could not say yet if she had suffered a concussion. He also mentioned that the brutal act seemed to be intentional because no purse or contents were stolen from her. Edna will remain in intensive care for the time being, where she will be given all the treatment she needs. That was all about he could tell them and the next twenty-four hours were critical.

Two police detectives showed up and started asking questions, but no one could tell what happened.

"We are here to investigate an attempted murder", one of them said. "Does she have any enemies?"

"Not that I know of", Richard answered. She is a hard working person that everyone loves, and she always shows consideration to people around her. She is not capable to do harm to anyone."

"What is your name and what is your relation with her?"

"Richard Werner, and we are going to get married. These are her parents."

"We'll find the truth, sooner or later, Mr. Werner", the detective said, and they both left.

Richard was in a deplorable state, and he only could say with a trembling voice to Debra and Glen:

"I'll stay for the night, and you two go home. I'll keep you posted."

Left alone, Richard sat down in an armchair trying to put his emotions in order.

A horrible thought flashed through his mind: 'If this act of cruelty was perpetrated by Mona? It means then that her intention was to kill Edna. Is such a thing possible? Mona is capable of many bad things, but getting to the murder is hard to believe, although it is possible.' Heavy thoughts flowed through Richard's mind, unable to control them. If Mona initiated this act of cruelty, she will not stop until she completes it by killing. Edna was in imminent danger and had to hide, but where, and how? Richard could find no answer to his questions, nor did he have anyone to consult with. He could not ask for the protection of the police, saying what his suspicions were because they might be wrong. He will wait until Edna recovers, and then they will both make a decision. Until then, he will protect her, always being close to her, and watching everyone who will approach her.

Richard was troubled by his thoughts and could not fall asleep. In the morning, the doctor told him that Edna was conscious but too weak to speak and he only was allowed to see her for no more than two minutes. She had no concussion, which was a very good sign. When Richard saw her, tears came to his eyes and he could hardly control them. Edna had a swollen face and all around her were all kinds of tubes that measured her vital signs. She could not speak but only tried to smile. Richard took her hand and kissed it, saying:

"The doctor told me that the baby is fine, and you'll get well. Edna and Glen came as soon as they heard about your accident."

The nurse approached and interrupted the conversation.

"I'm always by your side", Richard added. "Don't forget how much I love you."

He left the room and saw the two detectives who had not received approval from the doctor to interrogate Edna.

"I'm very worried about her life," Richard told them.

"We'll put a police officer at her door, for your peace of mind and ours. He will be there for the first shift and replaced with another one, so that she will be guarded twenty-four hours. We have to interrogate her, but the doctor did not allow us today. Maybe tomorrow."

Richard waited until the police officer showed up and saw him at Edna's door, then he went home to change and have a little rest. He placed with the police a big amount of money as a reward for any information regarding Edna's attacker.

After a few days, Edna felt better and had a long conversation with Richard about what they we'll do when she will leave the hospital. They both suspected that the attack had been carried out by someone Mona hired, but neither wanted to mention her name.

"It is not yet clear why you were attacked, and until the situation is clarified, you are still in danger. My opinion is not to wait until the police solve the case but to take protective measures in advance. Do you know what I'm suggesting? I suggest it would be good for both of us to go abroad for good."

"I think it is the safest solution, indeed. I would choose Paris, if you agree with me. There, we'll be able to take everything from the beginning, we'll be able to work, and have a beautiful family."

"Wonderful! Paris will be! When you leave the hospital, we'll apply for passports, get what we need, and leave without much regret, except for your parents."

"They will certainly understand and approve of us, knowing that we'll always keep in touch with them."

They both felt more relieved and the plan they thought about gave them the strength to go further on with confidence.

After a few days, Edna was moved to the recovery room and started feeling much better. Two days passed and Richard didn't show up. The next morning, Glen came by, trying to hide his emotions and searching for the right words to tell her:

"The gallery burned down and Richard was arrested for suspicion of arson."

Edna was horrified. She started trembling and couldn't make a sound. Glen continued pausing between his words:

"The police investigated asking questions around, and a man said that he saw Richard getting inside the gallery, and when he came out the fire exploded. He then was taken to the police station and I'll go now and find out what happened to him. You stay calm please, because I think he was framed and the truth will surface up."

Edna managed to put some words together:

"I want to go home, Glen. Take me out of here. I cannot stay and wait without knowing what happened."

"I talked to the doctor before I came to see you, and he said that it will be at least one week until you'll be released. I'll come over and tell you all about. Debra is terribly worried and has to manage alone only with Becky the work in the diner."

Edna was enraged this time. She was convinced that Mona hired someone to burn down her gallery and framed Richard for arson. She was ready to go to the police and tell them about that awful woman who threatened her and who promised to do everything to take Richard back. For the time being, Edna was incapacitated in that hospital bed and could do nothing but wait. Her mind was like a storm and first, she had to sort out her thoughts carefully.

Next day, Glen told Edna that he couldn't see Richard but he waited outside for his lawyer and spoke with him. He said that "the District Attorney filed charges and the preliminary hearing will be in a couple of days. After that, Richard will go to trial and we'll see what happens next."

"I'll go to court and testify in his defense, Glen."

Edna told him all about Mona and how she threatened her not long ago. Glen didn't know anything about that woman and got scared.

"It's not a good choice, Edna. If you show up in court, you expose yourself to big danger and no one could help you. I advise you to wait and see what Richard's lawyer will do in his defense. When you'll be ready to leave the hospital, I'll take you to stay with us and hide for a while. We have enough space in our apartment above the diner, and you'll be comfortable and safe. There is nothing to do for now."

"I think you're right, Glen, and I don't want to make things even worse. Thank you for everything you do for me, and I appreciate a lot yours and Debra's care for me. We just have to wait for the time being, at least until I'll be released."

At the arraignment, Richard pleaded "not guilty" and the judge scheduled his trial to begin after two weeks.

In a few days, Edna was released and the doctor gave her all the instructions to follow, including medication and therapy. Glen helped her to take her belongings and to move as they both decided. Debra was happy to have her around and made everything for Edna to be comfortable. She told them both about the decision she took with Richard, to go to Paris where they would be safe and Mona could not find them. Both Debra and Glen found difficult to accept this solution but considered it to be the most suitable. For the time being, Edna decided to leave alone if Richard was convicted; she will wait for him no matter how long the sentence lasts until he will be able to join her. In the following days, Edna applied for a passport, which she will receive after two weeks. As for the money, she had enough to ensure her existence for a few months abroad, and her insurance policy was good enough to pay compensations that would be very helpful for the situation she was in. At the trial, the prosecutor called as witness the same man who said he recognized Richard when he came out of the building before the fire started. It took only one hour for the jury to decide for guilty verdict, and Richard was sentenced to three years in prison.

After few days, Edna went to see him, and at first, they both started crying and then took the phone and talked looking at each other through the glass partition between them. He was allowed only ten minutes, so both told quickly what happened to them lately.

"You took the right decision to go away, even if for me is an excruciating pain for not knowing anything about you."

"My parents will keep you informed about every move I'll make there. I'll wait for you, for as long as it will take to join me and our baby, and be together. I cannot live without you."

Time for the visit was over and Edna had to leave, knowing that for a long time they will be apart and both will feel miserable.

After a couple of days, Edna booked a night flight to Paris. Before anything, she went to her bank and transferred her money to the same branch in Paris, keeping only a small amount in her purse. She took only two suitcases with a few of her belongings, her camera, some samples of her work, and Richard's portrait.

It was time for her to bit farewell from Debra and Glen, whom she dearly called "her parents", who saved her life, and were always there for her with their love and care. With tears in their eyes, they made each other promises to stay in touch and be close as always.

Edna boarded the plane, leaving behind the places she knew, the people she cherished, and the man who meant for her more than her life.

Chapter 3

Afterward

The plane landed at Charles de Gaulle Airport after eleven hours of flying. It was Thursday morning at eight o'clock when Edna got off and headed for the baggage claim area. She unfolded her small luggage cart and placed her two suitcases, heading for customs area. It was the beginning of February, the weather was very cold, but Edna had warm winter clothes and boots. The customs officer looked at Richard's portrait and said:

"This must be expensive, do you have approval papers for it?"

"I made it and I don't need approval. It has my signature."

The officer compared her signature with the passport, and let her go. After checking with customs, and passing through screening, she tried to give a phone call to her parents, but her cell phone was out of range, so she headed to a phone booth, and asked for a call collect. It was five o'clock in the afternoon there, and Debra answered. When she heard Edna's voice, she screamed with joy, but Edna interrupted her, saying that she arrived well, but couldn't tell everything, so that they wouldn't pay too much for the call. She told Debra that she was on her way to the hotel and will call from there after she will check in.

The hotel was inside the terminal, right above the train station; following the signs, it took Edna only twenty minutes walk to get to the hotel entrance. She went inside a big hall, and headed straight to the desk where a young girl received her smiling, asking her in English what she could do for her. Edna replied in impeccable French that she wanted a room for maybe a week to stay. The girl seemed delighted and asked her if she had any preference, to which Edna replied that she had none, just a comfortable room. She signed the papers, and the girl called the bellhop who took her luggage and led her to the elevator, and then to a room on the second floor, very comfortable and elegant. Edna gave him a good tip; he bowed and asked her if she needed anything else.

"What is your name?"

"Jean."

"I would like you, Jean, to bring me a detailed map of the city, and some local papers and magazines."

"With pleasure, Madame."

He came back in less than ten minutes.

"Madame would like to have room service?"

"No, Jean, thank you. I'll go downstairs and have my meals there."

"Very well, Madame. Enjoy your stay."

He left and Edna started unpacking and thinking what to do next. She remembered to call Edna or Glen and giving them a detailed rapport about her journey. It was already noontime, but not too late; she placed a long distance call from the room phone and Glen answered. Edna told him everything about her journey, saying that she will start maybe tomorrow looking for a place to live and a job.

"Have you seen Richard? How is he?"

"Hanging in there and trying to be strong. We talked a lot about you and how much we all miss you. Tomorrow I'll go and tell him the news and make him feel better."

"Tell him not to forget his promises and that I'll wait for him for as long as it takes. I'll call you when I'll make some arrangements and I'll find a little easier my ways around here. Give my love to Debra and Richard. My love to you too. Bye, Glen, until I'll call you again."

It was passed noon already and Edna was hungry. She went downstairs to the dining room and had a good meal, and then she visited the gift shop close by. A small brief case attracted her attention and that was exactly what she needed for her portfolio; she bought it with credit card and went back to her room. All afternoon she spent checking the magazines and newspapers. She found out some addresses of fashion agencies which she intended to contact for a job. Before anything, Edna needed a place to live, and for that she found several addresses and chose one which according to the map, seemed to be in a neighborhood where public transportation was most accessible. It was a one bedroom apartment, with all utilities paid in a modern five-story building.

Next morning, she asked for a cab which was already at the door when she came downstairs. First of all, she needed a phone and a laptop.

The cab driver asked in English:

"Where to?"

Edna told him in French to take her to an electronic shop.

"Madame has a beautiful Parisian accent. Is Madame on vacation in France?"

"Yes, and I hope to enjoy it."

"My name is Antoine, here is my card, and Madame can call me anytime for service."

"Thank you, Antoine, you are of big help."

(These French people are stepping on my nerves with their manners and politeness, she thought.)

They arrived at the shop and Edna said:

"Wait for me, Antoine."

Once inside, she saw a big display of electronic devices, TVs, and phones. She asked for an iPhone and a laptop. The vendor showed her several models, recommending the ones with best operating systems. Edna made her choice and asked him to configure both of them so that they could be used abroad; it took him only a few minutes to connect and to configure both of them; he gave her a number for the iPhone and the access to internet for both. Edna paid with credit card; she entered the car, and told Antoine to take her to the address of the apartment, telling him to wait for her. At the desk, a corpulent woman in her fifties, was the manager; she introduced herself by the name Vicki Lambert; she greeted Edna with a smile and showed her the apartment located at the third floor; the front side of the building was on a busy street, but the apartment was at the back of the building, with no street nearby, and overlooked a fairly large park. It also had a small storage room next to the kitchen, which Edna could use as dark room. She didn't like it too much; it had not enough light coming from the windows, the carpet looked quite used, and the kitchen was too small.

"I have to think about and I'll let you know my decision", Edna said.

"I have a two bedroom apartment on the same floor, at the right corner of the building; it is ready for rent, but I didn't have time to list it in the paper. Would you like to see it?"

"Certainly."

That one was much better. It had a bigger bedroom and one smaller, the kitchen was large enough, and next to it was a small dining area; the carpet was new, and all the rooms had plenty of light. It also had a storage room like the other one. From the corner windows of the big bedroom, Edna could see part of the street, and also the park on the back side.

"This is much better, and I like it. First, I'll take some picture to buy the right size of the furniture."

She took pictures with the iPhone, from each corner and sides of the walls.

"I'm glad you like it", Mme Lambert said. "We can go downstairs and sign the agreement."

Her husband was at the desk and was pleased with Edna's decision. The rent was a bit high, but worth the price. Edna signed the lease, and paid with credit card the first month rent.

"I'll order the furniture today and everything I need for the household, asking to be delivered as soon as possible. Everything should be placed in the apartment. Please call me at the hotel and leave a message when they'll arrive."

"Yes, Mme Mathis, it is a pleasure to have you as a tenant and I'll call as you asked."

The next step was to her bank. When Edna introduced herself to the manager, he smiled, checked her records, and was very pleased with the large amount of money she transferred to his branch. Edna gave him her address, phone number, and asked for checkbooks and some cash. He gave her what she needed, and smiled again when she left.

Next, Edna told Antoine to take her to a furniture store, where she also could find all she needed for her household. She showed the vendor the pictures of the apartment, who sent them to his computer; then she chose everything and got a good price; this time, she paid with check.

"For today, we finished, Antoine, but maybe tomorrow or the day after I'll need a ride."

"Madame has my phone number and I'll be very pleased to be at Madame's service."

Edna paid him more than he asked for, and he was extremely pleased.

It was late afternoon when she got back at the hotel. First thing, Edna began to make all the calculations for the expenses she had made that day, and found them quite acceptable. She felt tired after all she solved in that day, was hungry, and went downstairs for dinner. It was not the right time for calling Debra and Glen, so she decided to call them in the morning. Back in her room, Edna checked the internet, and found a company providing a very inexpensive program for abroad calls; she subscribed, thinking that she could save a lot of money. In that night, she slept without dreams and without many of the worries, she had before.

The next morning, Edna called Debra and Glen on her iPhone, telling them everything she did the day before. From now on, they could see each other on the small screen either on the laptop or on the iPhone. Debra and Glen had both possibilities and they knew how to use them easily; they all opened the small screen seeing each other for the first time since Edna left. The reunion was emotional and Debra began to cry. Glen had visited Richard the day before and always brought him news from Edna; next time he has more to tell him. Richard thought only of her, and it seemed that this was the only way he could withstand imprisonment. Debra and Glen were both competing for stories, and their life at diner was unchanged. Their only pleasure and comfort was to talk to her and from now on they will have great joy in seeing her. They could call her easily, but they didn't know her schedule, so Edna had to call them when she could. They took pictures of each other and promised to talk next day.

The following afternoon, Edna got the message from Mme Lambert saying that everything in her apartment was ready and she could come anytime. Edna called Antoine in the next day; he drove her to the apartment and waited for her. She went upstairs, accompanied by Mme Lambert, and was very pleased. Everything was in the right place and looked just the way she liked.

"Everything looks very good. Tomorrow I'll move in, and thank you Mme Lambert for your kindness."

"The pleasure is mine, Mme Mathis."

She asked Antoine to pick her up next day, around noon, from the hotel. She packed her things, paid the hotel bills, and when Antoine showed up, Edna was ready to go home.

First thing she did, was to place Richard's portrait above her bed, and the jade figurine on the night table. The small bedroom she intended to use for working on her paintings. Then she checked the appliances and every detail around. From the living room she could step outside into a small balcony from where she could admire the large park in front of her. Edna was very pleased. She made pictures of almost every side of the apartment and sent them to Debra and Glen. One of them was Richard's portrait above her bed. She was hungry, and from the nearby store she bought a lot of food. A bookstore was close by, and she bought some literature books and magazines. In that night she could sleep easier, in her own bed, in her own home.

Next morning, she took lots of pictures and sent them to Debra and Glen with the message *this is my home waiting for my beloved Richard.* She intended to have a long walk and get familiar with the neighborhood, but it was snowing and very cold. She liked a lot her home; everything there was the way she even not expected to be so cozy and comfortable. Edna thought about looking for a job, but the weather was very bad and she had to wait.

In that day she talked a lot with Debra and Glen who both were amazed how well she managed to solve her problems. After a week, the weather improved and Edna could make short walks in her neighborhood; she liked a lot everything around. Both, the subway and bus stations were at the corner of her street; stores and boutiques showed a big display of merchandise for every taste and need; people walked back and forth the streets and looked busy going to work or shopping.

Edna thought it was time to be checked by a doctor. She searched the internet for a reputable clinic and found a hospital that was recommended as one of the most prestigious in the city. She consulted the map and easily found the address; it wasn't too far and she decided to take the subway. She made an appointment and after two days she went to the clinic, where a young lady doctor consulted her and did a sonogram. Her pregnancy was in a very early stage, but the sonogram showed everything that could be seen.

"It's a boy," the doctor said, and showed her all the details as explicitly as possible.

Edna was at the height of her happiness and could no longer contain the many questions she had. The doctor told her that the pregnancy was progressing very well and made many recommendations that Edna had to follow. She gave her a copy of the sonogram and scheduled her in a month for the next visit.

Back home, first thing Edna did, was to send the sonogram to Debra and Glen, asking them to show it to Richard.

"I don't think is a good idea", Glen said.

"Why?"

"He might do something foolish, like trying to escape and end up with more years in prison. With the approval of the guard who was watching, we showed him the pictures of your home, and he became excited like ready to explode when he read the texting. If we show him the sonogram, he will not be able to take it easy. It's much better for him not to see it."

Edna understood and thought they were right. She missed to share with him the greatest happiness she ever had.

It was already the beginning of March, the weather was warming up and it was time for Edna to look for work. In art magazines and local newspapers, no fashion or modeling agency had published any job application for professional photographers. On the internet, Edna took information about every modeling and fashion agency in town and made a list starting with the most famous and ending with the lesser known. Since none of them had published any employment ad, Edna decided to introduce herself directly and try an interview with the respective Art Director. For start, Edna considered the fashion agency first on her list. She checked her portfolio in her briefcase, and the next morning, elegantly dressed, Edna went to the agency, asking to speak to the Art Director. The waiting room was empty; the secretary told her that he does not receive solicitors for jobs without an appointment; she asked Edna what was the problem she came for. Edna told her that she came for a personal conversation and would wait until he will receive her. She sat down in an armchair and began to browse the magazines lined up on the table. After almost two hours, the door opened and a man in his fifties, with gray hair and a beard, appeared in the doorway and looked at Edna for a couple of minutes:

"Do you want a meeting with me?"

"I would really appreciate you giving me a few minutes of your time."

"Come in."

He showed her an armchair, asking only why she came for, without requesting her name and without recommending himself.

"I would like to work as a professional photographer in your agency."

"What references do you have?"

Edna didn't answer, but instead, opened the briefcase and lined up the photos and sketches one by one until they covered the entire desk. He looked at them intently and in astonishment, rising his eyebrows, and without saying a word. After a while, he said:

"Very interesting and well done, but during this period we do not hire; maybe later. What is your name?"

"Edna Mathis."

"I'm Louis Dermont. When we'll start hiring, I'll let you know, Mlle Mathis. Here's my card, and when you leave, give your phone number to the secretary. It was a pleasure meeting you and seeing your work. Good day."

"Good day, Monsieur Dermont."

Edna did not expect to be hired from the first interview, so she did not lose her courage at all. There were fifteen more agencies on her list, and if necessary, she would try them all. The next day, she set off again for the second agency on her list, which was also promoting models. The wait this time was shorter, for only an hour, after which she was called to the Art Director's office. A woman in her forties, with beautiful features, who had probably once been a model, received Edna with a smile.

"I am Simone Blanchard. What is your name and what is the purpose of the visit?"

"Edna Mathis, and I would appreciate a few minutes of your time for an interview about the possibility of a job as a professional photographer."

"As I can see, you should rather be a model, not a photographer, Mlle Mathis. What references do you have?"

"I was once a model. Here are my works as a photographer and illustrator."

Edna lined up all again the pictures and sketches in front of her on the desk. Madame Blanchard looked at them carefully and analyzed them with a magnifying glass, looking for every detail that interested her. After a while, she said:

"Excellent, Mlle Mathis. I can see the work of a professional here. You also developed the films?"

"Yes, Madame."

"Next week will be the inauguration of a new fashion line. Until then, you will get acquainted with the way we work here. As a first test, you will start photographing some models tomorrow, which will be chosen to pose for you, and you will show your expertise in art and film development. An assistant will be at your disposal for as long as you work. If your work will be at the same level as the photographs you showed me, I will hire you and you'll start working for the opening line. Do you agree?"

"Wonderful Mme Blanchard. Thank you for the confidence you show me."

"Be here tomorrow morning at nine o'clock."

Edna started singing on the street, on the way back home. The next morning at nine o'clock sharp, wearing a denim overall, she was already handling the camera and taking pictures of the model posing for her on the stage. A girl assisted her, moving around as fast as Edna asked her, changing films and cameras and barely breathing. Three models, one after the other, changed dresses and posed on stage in a variety of looks; Edna asked them all the time how to move and how to show their best features. After about seven hours, Edna went to the dark room and developed the films. She was very pleased with her work. It was already nine o'clock when she finished, and everyone left already long before. The next morning, Edna was there, took the pictures she chose, and showed them to Mme Blanchard.

"To tell you the truth, I'm amazed not only by the work you did, but also by the way you did it. The test given to you was to measure not only your talent, but also your speed and your behavior. Mlle Mathis, you past the test with great success. Congratulations, Edna, and please call me Simone!"

"Thank you kindly, Simone. This means that I'm hired?"

"With flowers! Tomorrow you'll start the photo shoot for the opening line. Here is your salary for the beginning. Now you can go home and relax."

Edna was amazed when she saw the salary she will be paid with; it was much above of all her expectations.

After one week, she received a call from Monsieur Dermont:

"I would like you to come over and discuss the contract for your job."

"I have a job already."

"Who hired you?"

"One of your competitors who liked my work and my attitude."

"I'll pay you twice."

"You can pay me ten times and my answer would be the same. I rather like to be loyal to my employer. Good day, Monsieur Dermont."

By the end of March, the fashion line opened at Carrousel du Louvre, the impressive building with the upside-down pyramid near the entrance of the Louvre museum. The success was huge, with outstanding reviews in the most publicly acknowledged fashion magazines.

The next exhibition will be in fall, and until then, Edna had plenty of time to do what she liked most, namely, walking the streets, taking pictures of people and then painting them. After the great success of the line, a lot of girls turned to the agency to be portrayed and promoted as models. Simone called Edna:

"We now have a relaxing time until fall when we'll start working for the new line. Until then, you will photograph these girls who aspire to glory and fame, but you will not work more than four hours a day, and maybe not even that. You'll be paid on commission, and make your schedule the way you like."

Edna was very pleased with that assignment, since she had plenty of time to do her own work.

During the summer, she managed to build an appreciable collection of photographs, after which she made sketches and paintings. For the time being, she placed them all in the small bedroom, sorting them by composition, thinking that sometime much later, she will be able to open her own gallery.

Edna began to think that the time to give birth was approaching. She moved all the paintings in the dark room and made all the necessary preparations in the small bedroom that she transformed into a nursery, thinking that she will need a live-in nanny.

At the beginning of October, the signs of giving birth appeared to be close. One morning, Edna urgently needed to go to the hospital, and went downstairs where Mrs. Lambert immediately understood the situation, offering to drive her there.

That evening, Edna gave birth to a beautiful baby boy. Her happiness rose to the heavens when she saw him and the nurse put him in her arms. Her doctor asked:

"Do you have someone at home to take care of him? I know you're working and you don't need help yet since you'll stay home for a while, but you'll need it later."

"I would like to hire a skilled nanny who will be with him all the time, but I don't know anyone. I'll have to look for one and I don't know where."

"I might have someone who has been working here for many years in the pediatric unit, and who would love to change her job with something easier and better paid."

The doctor called her, and a woman in her early fifties or even younger, appeared in the room; she was short, plump, with a round face and round eyes.

"This is Linette Blanc", the doctor said, "and now I leave you both to talk and come to an agreement."

"I'm glad to meet you, Linette; the doctor warmly recommended you. My name is Edna Mathis and I would like to hire you as a live-in nanny. Can you tell me a little about your background?"

She said that she was originally from Cherbourg, where she was born and raised without leaving the town for many years not even going to the neighboring town. In her youth she had a daughter, Martine, out of wedlock, whom she raised, working as a registered nurse at the hospital. After the girl grew up and got married, she didn't get along with her son in law, and decided to leave and change the way of life she had until then. She moved to Paris and worked in the children's ward at the hospital ever since. She managed to know the city in details, and she satisfied her desire to see the beauty and richness of this beautiful city. However, the time has come to have a quieter and more secure life; she will be happy to work as a nanny for Edna and her baby, mentioning a salary that was usually paid for that job. Edna seemed very pleased with the explanation and offered her a much higher pay than she asked for and a day off at her choice.

After a few days, Edna, the baby, and Linette, went home. Mme Lambert and her husband greeted them with a big smile.

"This is the third baby born in the last year in our building. The other two are girls", she said. "Congratulations and best wishes."

"Thank you both, very much", Edna answered.

They entered the apartment, and Linette made her first remark:

"Smells oil paint."

"This is because I paint."

"Well, you won't paint from now on. It's unhealthy for the baby. Where is the nursery?"

Edna showed her, she placed the baby asleep in the crib, and started inspecting every corner in the apartment.

"We need to buy some things."

"Make a list and I'll buy whatever you say."

After a few minutes, Linette showed her two pages with what she called 'were very important'.

"I'll go now and buy them", Edna said.

"No. You stay with the baby, watch him, and don't move until I'll be back, probably in an hour."

"Take a cab and here is the money, which probably will be enough."

Edna felt tired and hungry. The baby was asleep and she prepared something for lunch. Linette returned after more than an hour, helped by the cab driver who carried at least ten bags and packages. She unpacked them and put everything in place, as if she knew well how to get around.

"You must be hungry. I made lunch and let's eat. The baby is sleeping."

"Let's see what a cook you are Mme Mathis."

"Call me 'Edna', since we both have a long way to go together."

"All right, Edna, I don't want to intrude or be nosy, but I would like to know a bit about you."

Edna told her about her life without hiding any unpleasant times she went through. She thought that it would be better for Linette to know the truth about her.

"You had a terribly hard life, Edna. You think that he'll come to join you and the baby?"

"I only can hope for the best, Linette. Now, I would like to take a nap and rest a little bit; I feel tired. You do whatever you want, rest a little bit, or watch TV."

Edna woke up in the evening; she heard Linette singing a lullaby and went straight to the nursery.

"Did you rest well? You must be hungry, I cooked, but you have first to feed the baby."

She gave Edna to breastfeed him and in the same time, she set the table.

"Did you think about a name for him?"

"*Aden,* after Richard's father."

"Beautiful!"

The baby fell asleep in Edna's arms, Linette put him in his crib, and they could have diner. Edna said:

"We know each other only for a few hours, but I must say that you are a blessing, Linette."

"You are too, Edna. You took me in, and gave me the home I always wished to have."

"In about two weeks the new line will open and I must start working in a couple of days. I'll be out from early morning till late evening. Will you be comfortable with my schedule?"

"You have nothing to worry about. Aden and I we'll do just fine. We both understand very well one another. Now, you go back to sleep and have a good rest."

"May I leave the door open?"

Linette gave her a long look and said:

"Leave the door open and I'll leave mine too. Are you scared?"

"No. I just want to feel you both close to me. Good night, Linette."

"Good night, dear."

Next morning, after feeding the baby, and having breakfast with Linette, Edna started sketching both. It took her about two hours, but she had to follow Linette from place to place since she didn't have time to pose.

"I'll frame it and keep it on my night table", Edna said.

"It's awesome. Make me one too."

"Tomorrow. Now, I have to talk with my parents and I want you to take Aden and show your faces on the small screen."

Both Edna and Glen started crying and took many pictures.

"I wish Richard could see his son, but I don't know if we should tell him", Glen said.

"If you allow me", Linette said, "I would suggest that it will do him good, and this will be the best medication for him. Don't worry that he will get too excited; he will cry softly first, and then he'll have peace in his soul; this will keep him live with big hopes to join them both. I know a father's mind in any kind of situations, and believe me, he will react just the way I predicted."

"Thank you Linette", Debra said, "you seem to have a big experience about human nature, and you are much wiser than the three of us."

"We'll go tomorrow and see him", Glen said. We'll show him all the pictures we took, and I'll call you back. Nice meeting you, Linette. Bye now."

It seemed that Linette was right, because Richard reacted just as she predicted.

After two weeks, the opening was again a huge success, where the cream of fashion industry met and struck deals at unbelievable high prices. Edna took many pictures and showed them to Linette, saying that a little bit of that glamour was her contribution too.

"People, actually buy these dresses?"

"At very high prices."

"I don't even like them and I wouldn't buy any of them."

"They are not your size, Linette, and not even mine anymore, but they are in high demand. Very rich designers sell them to even richer buyers who after a little while, trash them and wait for the next line. This is the way the fashion industry runs."

Edna had enough time to relax, be around her baby, and do some of her work; the weather outside was cold, it was snowing and she had to stay only inside.

A week before Christmas, Edna wanted to buy and decorate a tree, in celebration for the holiday; she asked Linette where to find it.

"You live in this city for almost a year and you don't know more than the next street."

"I had to work, and never had time for touristic sightseeing. Just tell me where to go."

"I'll go and you watch Aden."

She returned after almost two hours, with a beautiful medium-sized tree and decorations.

Three days before Christmas, Edna started to decorate the tree in the living room, Aden was sleeping and Linette was in the kitchen preparing lunch, when the laptop rang. Edna opened it and froze. She only could find little energy to whisper:

"Richard…"

"I'm coming home, my dear love."

Edna was unable to articulate a sound. She barely managed to ask:

"When?"

"I'll take a night flight tomorrow and I'll be there the next morning. I can't wait to see you both. Just say something! I'm alive and I've been released yesterday!"

"How?"

"I'll tell you all about when I'll be there. Be happy for me and for the three of us!"

Little by little Edna begun to recuperate from her shock.

"Am I dreaming or are you for real?", she asked.

"Look at me! Can't you see how happy I am? I'll tell you all when I'll meet you there. I must go now."

Edna came completely out of her shock:

"I'll meet you at the airport. Wear winter clothes because it's cold and snowing. I can't wait to see you and to tell you how much I missed you."

"Me too. Can I see my boy?"

"He is sleeping now. Come quickly and don't waste any time."

"I will. Bye my love.

"Bye dearest."

She run to the kitchen and this time, the words were competing to come out of her mouth and her voice turned to high pitch.

"Oooo...slow down, and speak quietly. Don't let your excitement to overwhelm you. Here, take a glass of water."

Edna jumped and kissed Linette on both cheeks.

"I'm going to the airport to meet him in the morning. I would like you to order the best food in town to be delivered, so we don't have to cook lunch. I'm sure you'll like him a lot and he'll like you too..."

"Did you finish?"

"I'll never finish talking about him."

"Now, be a good girl and finish decorating the tree, then come to the nursery and feed your baby. After that we'll eat lunch."

That morning, Edna left for the airport and arrived just as the plane landed. She waited impatiently for almost two hours at the bottom of the stairs, watching every one passing on the platform above, while waiting for Richard to appear. The passengers were descending the stairs, in a hurry to get out of the airport as soon as possible. Finally, she saw him as he began to descend the stairs, handling his two suitcases. Edna was impatient, but she was not allowed to cross the bottom of the stairs. When he reached the last step, Edna jumped in his arms, he held her tightly close to his chest, kissing each other again and again; they confused all the traffic, forcing the passengers to go around that pair that seemed to be unable to move.

"Let me look at you and make sure I don't dream", he said. "You are even more beautiful than before if this could be possible."

"You are pale and you lost weight, but you kept the beauty, the voice, and the elegance with which you conquered me. I can't even believe so much happiness. Let's get out of here as people start to get nervous. Let's go home, my love."

"I have to call Debra and Glen first. I don't know how I could have survived without them."

He talked to both for a few minutes and promised to call them later.

Arriving in the hall of the building, the Lamberts kindly received Richard after Edna introduced him as her husband. Linette opened the door, greeted him with a friendly smile, and invited him inside. Richard got directly to the point:

"Linette, because we are all a family here, I would like us to call each other by the first name from the beginning. Do you agree? "

"Completely. I've already started to like you."

"I'd like to wash first, and then see my son."

"I'm starting to like you even more, Richard," Linette said, pointing to the bathroom.

"Was the food delivered?" Edna asked.

"Come and see."

The dinette table was covered with all kinds of goodies and arranged for lunch.

"He is awfully handsome", Linette said.

"I know."

Richard came out of the bathroom and they both accompanied him to the nursery. Aden was cooing, making all kind of sounds, and had fun moving his hands and feet.

"He is a miracle and it's almost like a dream that I'm going through. Can I hold him? "

Linette handed him the baby and Richard couldn't get enough of looking at him and kissing his little hands.

"He's a big boy; how old is he now?"

"About eleven weeks, but he is much stronger than a baby usually is at his age", Edna said. "Now, let's go and have lunch and talk if you feel like."

"I have to give him the bottle with his formula, because he is hungry. "If you want, you can unpack and then have lunch," Linette said.

Richard took his suitcases and Edna led him into the bedroom. He was very pleasantly surprised by his portrait above the bed and the jade figurine on the nightstand. He took the jade figurine representing the girl out of his pocket and placed it on the other nightstand.

"Do you remember? It was about this time a year ago up in the mountains, "Richard said. "It's a dear anniversary now for us."

He took her in his arms holding her warmly to his chest, and saying:

"I love you so much it's almost painful. Aden and you are my whole life. "

"I know, I feel the same way."

He took out of his suitcase the self-portrait she painted for him, and she remembered him saying that he will always keep it close to him.

"Place it next to mine. I like to see them side by side."

"You'll do that; now let's go eat. You must be hungry."

"Very. I saw lot of good food on the table; do you eat every day like that?"

"You wish. Linette ordered it especially for you; otherwise, we both cook. After lunch you'll tell us the story of your release."

They all showed a big appetite talking only about Aden and his behavior. After finishing lunch, they sat in the living room with a cup of coffee, and Richard started his story:

"Long after my incarceration, the police caught the arsonist who was a professional and was employed by various people who asked for his service and who paid him to set fire either for a criminal purpose, or to collect money from insurance. On the occasion of such an incident, the arsonist was caught. Squeezed by the police, he admitted that he set many fires, including the gallery. He was hired by Mona who paid him a large sum of money to set fire to the gallery and erase any traces that would have led to her. In exchange for his testimony, the arsonist was convicted to a lesser punishment. The witness who claimed to have seen me leaving the building was brought back to court and testified that he was also hired and paid by Mona to testify at the trial against me. A little later, a man presented himself to the police asking for the promised reward for information about your attack. He testified that he was hidden in the car parked next to yours, saw the whole scene, and managed to memorize the face of the person who attacked you. He didn't intervene because he feared for his life. The police displayed in front of him an album with pictures of the criminals who were wanted for the crimes committed and who were known in advance. The witness immediately recognized the figure of your attacker, and after a while, the criminal was caught. The police rewarded the witness, but called him to trial to testify under oath in my favor. At the trial, the attacker said he was paid by Mona to kill you, but did not have enough time to complete the murder because people begun to appear around him. Mona was arrested for arson and attempted murder. She was trialed and sentenced to ten years in prison, without the possibility of parole; I was released after a week with an apology from the court and the authorities. While I was in prison, my attorney filed for my divorce, and shortly after, it came through. When I got out of there, I went straight to your parents, and they helped me with everything I had to do. I liquidated everything, my passport was valid, I transferred the money to the branch in Paris, I packed my suitcases, and run toward life and light, and you, and my baby, trying to forget the horrible ordeal I've been through."

After a few moments of silence, Edna said:

"I like when all the pieces fall in places, and the jigsaw puzzle displays the entire colorful design, anticipated with all the shades of best choices and right decisions."

"What goes around comes around", Linette added.

That night, Richard had nightmares, trembled, and could not sleep at all. Edna held him in her arms, trying to calm him down but only managed for a few minutes. He was troubled by the sufferings endured in the last year that were repeated in his mind, tormenting him subconsciously.

In the morning, Edna proposed a walk that would have been good for both of them. The weather was pleasant, people were on holiday, and the shops were crowded with customers who stocked up for Christmas. A pleasant atmosphere was displayed everywhere giving everyone a feeling of gratitude. Walking without any special purpose, Edna and Richard arrived in front of a jewelry store.

"Know something? Let's buy the wedding rings and get married after Christmas ", Richard suggested.

"That will make me very happy."

They went inside, and chose what they liked from a rich selection, then asked the jeweler to engrave the word *forever* on both. On the way home, they bought some art albums, some music compact discs, and an iPhone for Richard. After almost two hours, they returned home, better off than they had left. They showed Linette the wedding rings and announced that they would get married after the holidays, without any special celebration.

"I want us to get married in church and Aden to be baptized", Edna said.

"I didn't know you are so religious."

"I'm not, and this has nothing to do with religion. My faith is based on logic and understanding the realities of Creation and not on superstitions and stories. You see, every human being needs a place called 'somewhere' to belong to, and that place is built by family, moral values, tradition, heredity, all the way to roots. Nobody chooses this place; it comes with birth. You had such a place, you grew up there, and you know the history of it; I didn't have one and I belonged to 'nowhere'. I didn't know my parents, who my ancestors were, and why I was rejected from my rights to belong to my real family. My mother chose such a place for me when she left me at the door of a convent. That door opened, but it could have stayed closed all the same. I was given there, a miniature replica of what I didn't was provided with; I grew up there, and understood that I was an orphan without a known birthday, and that place became the one where I belonged. I've learned to respect and honor it, and it became a part of my soul to stay with me for as long as I live. If I disregard it, there is nothing for me left to respect and honor concerning my ancestry and my roots, even if they were not the real ones. Part of my soul will remain empty and I'll become an outsider, feeling again that I belong nowhere. Now, I belong to my family that I cherish and means more than my life, but I took with me the replica of my ancestry, that I'll always respect and honor."

Richard and Linette were stunned.

"I said many times, and I'm saying it again: You never cease to amaze me. Never crossed my mind that this subject could be interpreted and analyzed the way you just described it."

"Everything you told us, makes a lot sense to me. As Richard said, never I thought that this subject could have such interpretation."

"Thank you both for understanding me."

They celebrated Christmas in a warm atmosphere, full of family enthusiasm, each expressing their wishes for the future to be fulfilled with joy and success. Debra and Glen also participated in the celebration together, hoping that one day they will have the happiness to see each other again.

After Christmas, Edna and Richard filed for civil marriage and obtained the license. She took the name *Edna Mathis-Werner*. In the following Sunday, the whole family went to the nearby church and first, the priest solemnized the marriage service; after the prayer and the reading, Richard and Edna exchanged vows and the wedding rings; then, the priest blessed the man and the woman who became united. After that, he officiated the baptism of Aden according to the Christian tradition.

"You feel better now?", Richard asked.

"Like never before. How do you feel?"

"The happiest man in the world."

"Nobody gives us any attention?", Linette asked.

They both embraced and kissed her and Aden by turn.

"Now, I'm happy too, and I wish you and Aden all the best in your life. Let's go home."

In that day, they listened to music, danced a little, and had lot of fun.

Next morning Richard said that he wanted to look for a job.

"Long ago, you wished to be a museum curator. There are many places where you can try, but don't start with the Louvre or Orsay."

She told him how she found her job, by going directly to the top, and not staying in line.

"I'll do that after New Year's Eve; until then I'll try to find some midsize museums and do some research online."

In that night, Edna was long asleep, while Richard tried to sort out the many thoughts that came into his mind. After many hours without any sleep, he knew exactly what he had to do.

"We go shopping", he said in the morning.

They went out when the bookstore opened, and Richard searched the art section. He selected almost twenty art books, albums, and art reference publications.

"What are you going to do with all these?"

"Study."

Back home, they took a cab; he placed all volumes and papers by subject, on the bed, on the floor, and on the desk in the corner. For a few days after that, he studied all the materials he had bought, taking notes and selecting the information that interested him. By turns, Edna and Linette brought him food, without asking questions, or disturbing him. In those few nights that followed, Edna slept on the couch in the living room, but it seemed that he didn't even notice.

"Are you already divorced?"

"Let him study, Linette. He aims high and he knows what he's doing."

The New Year's Eve was already there; he came out of the room to celebrate, and Edna asked him about the progress in his study.

"I'm confident, but I'm worried about you, because I gave you lot of trouble. Please bear with me for a little while."

"I'm behind you all the time to give you support for everything you need, no matter what the outcome will be. I'm convinced that you'll get the job you want."

After ten days, Richard left in the morning, with a briefcase filled with papers and a list of addresses.

After he left, Edna began to walk around the house without restraint; she was worried and with little hope, knowing that Richard had no references and without them, the chances of finding work were very low or not at all. Linette tried to calm her down, but without success. Just to make Edna get rid of the thoughts that were bothering her, she asked:

"What kind of job is he looking for?"

"Two possibilities that would interest him: a position as a museum curator, which is responsible for the collections of exhibits and the development of the way in which works of art can be interpreted through public displays and publications; he also provides information and design displays for the benefit of visitors. Second, he would like to find a so-called 'connoisseur' position that evaluates works of art in the style and technique of artists. The responsibility of the connoisseur is to assign the author, to validate the authenticity and to appreciate the quality. Richard is highly educated and very knowledgeable, but has no experience that might be required. However, I hope that he also has the power of persuasion and with that, he could take the job, which I'm sure he will appreciate and perform very well."

It was already ten o'clock in the evening when Richard returned home. As he opened the door, both Edna and Linette realized that he took the job. His face radiated joy, and he hugged them both, doing dance pirouettes around the living room.

"Tell us everything from the beginning, with all the details," Edna said, screaming with joy.

"I had three museum addresses that I considered. All three were at a great distance from each other, and I chose to go first to the one with the highest prestige of them. The director asked me for references and experiences, and I told him I didn't have any, but I showed him my Art Master degree. He told me it wasn't enough because he would have preferred someone with experience. I went to the next one considered prestigious, and the director questioned me in the same way, telling me that he has two more applicants and will make the decision in two weeks; if he chooses me he will call me. I was disappointed and with the few hopes I still had, I went to the third museum, called 'Petit Palais' which was smaller than the two before. The museum had a curator, but he was in his sixties and needed help. I answered a few questions that the director asked me, then he suggested that we take a look at the displays together to give me an overview. While visiting the exhibitions, he asked me various professional questions to which I answered correctly and with confidence. The museum is well known for its overview of European artistic masterpieces, which span from the medieval and renaissance periods to the end of the 19th century. It abounds in paintings, sculptures, and art objects from artists as diverse as *Rembrandt, Fragonard, Delacroix, Cézanne, Corot, Monet, Rodin, Pissarro* and many others. There is also a small but significant section dedicated to Roman and Greek art. It also hosts temporary exhibits that explore modern art, photography, and even fashion. After more than three hours, the director was satisfied with my answers and told me that he will give me the position of curator; the job requires forty working hours per week from ten-to-six, and some extra evenings and weekend, with Monday off; it is paid with a very good salary and benefits; he also said that I could watch the connoisseur at work and get experience, which can be useful in my job as curator. I'll start work on Tuesday morning. That is the whole story of today, and I must tell you that I'm very happy, and intend to show diligence, skill, and ambition to be at the expected level."

"Now, everybody can come to normal", Linette said. "You two go and eat, and I'll go to bed; I had enough excitement for one day. Good night."

It was late when they finished their meal and went to the bedroom where everything was a mess, with all his books and papers spread around.

"What are you going to do with all this stuff?"

"I need some more, because I have to read all the time."

"Am I supposed to move to the living room?"

"Oh, no my love. I'll try to clean up this mess and find a place for everything. I might need a bookcase and this will solve the problem."

"Tomorrow morning we'll go shopping."

In that night, Edna slept in her bed the first time in two weeks.

The next morning, they went to the furniture store and Richard chose a bookcase to hold about two hundred books. They asked to be delivered home, and then went to shop for food. The bookcase arrived after about two hours; they found a suitable place in the living room, and Richard organized all the books and materials he needed for study. At the same time, Edna talked to Debra and Glen, telling them everything that had happened lately, and they expressed their feelings of joy for all the successful accomplishments they reached.

"After two weeks I'll have to start working for the spring exhibition and I'll be busy from morning to evening. Lately, I haven't worked anything and I've missed it; the weather was bad to take pictures outside."

"You didn't paint at all. Why?", Richard asked.

"Linette does not allow because of the smell of oil. When the weather warms up, I can go out on the balcony and start painting again. Maybe much later, I'll have my gallery."

"I'll do my best to have everything you want, and be sure that you have all my support."

After a week working from morning to late evening, Richard managed to get to know every painting and artifact in the museum in addition to all the obligations required by his job. He also negotiated and authorized the purchase of a new collection of paintings that would arrive in a month. He was excited about his job even though he came home very tired. After a few days, Edna asked him:

"How long do you think you will last working day in and day out?"

"It won't be like that every day; I had to get acquainted from the beginning with the work and duties required by the job. It will be easier for me after I get used to it and I'll feel confident with everything I have to do."

"You don't even eat properly, and you don't know how fast your boy is growing up. He already does mini push ups, 'swimming' movements on his tummy, and rocking back and forth", Linette said.

"Please, both of you, don't lecture me. I eat at the café there, and I kiss my boy every time when

I come home, when he is asleep. What else can I do for the time being? In a while, everything will become normal."

The following week Edna began working on the spring line. From morning until late in the evening, she was at the agency photographing models and developing films. Returning home was difficult, having to take two buses and a subway line, which made her even more tired. Richard and Linette were waiting for her with impatience; they used to tell each other about everything they had done that day and showing their care as usually. At the end of the week, Richard came up with a proposal:

"I want to show you something that will please you. Linette, take Aden and come with me and Edna."

"Where?"

"Surprise."

They all went downstairs, and Richard led them to the garage where he showed them his new purchase; it was a new, small car that was aligned next to the other cars of the tenants. Edna and Linette opened their mouth to say something, but he said it first:

"I couldn't see you so tired coming from work taking the bus and the subway, and I couldn't bear you both carrying heavy bags of food from the store. This little car will make our lives easier and more pleasant for all of us. I'll drive you anywhere you need to go; I got my license last week and

I wanted to surprise you; please don't argue with me."

"This is marvelous", Edna said.

"I just love it!" Linette exclaimed.

"Splendid! Let's go for a drive; you pick the place.

"You two are highly educated and know the history of the city, but I know the places much better than you two; I would say Champs-Élysées, which is said to be the world's most beautiful avenue; the Arc de Triomphe is in the center of it."

All the way, Linette gave directions and it took Richard about twenty-five minutes to get there. While in the car, they talked and laughed and Aden seemed to have a very good time in Edna's arms.

"Where is this name coming from?", Linette asked.

"The origins of the 'Champs-Élysées' can be traced to 1640 when space was cleared to plant a line of trees, which would later become an avenue. The name translates to 'Elysian Fields' from the Greek mythology, meaning resting place of Greek gods and dead heroes, similar to the Christian paradise", Richard answered.

Edna and Richard exchanged their knowledge about the sites they were passing by.

"You two keep talking about culture; I want to learn something", Linette said.

They arrived at Place de la Concorde, situated at the end of the Champs-Élysées; it is famous for the Luxor Obelisk (**a** 3,300 year old Egyptian obelisk erected on the square in October 1836); it was the site of many notable public executions, including the executions of King Louis XVI and Marie Antoinette in the course of the French Revolution. The obelisk was placed to mark the spot where the guillotine stood during the French Revolution.

"It's late, and we should go home", Linette said.

After two weeks, the fashion line opened at the Carrousel du Louvre. Most of the photographs, Edna made at the *Tuileries Garden*, located just west of the Carrousel du Louvre. As backgrounds for the models were Aristide Maillol's statues and the likes of Rodin, and Henry Moore. Her models next to Auguste Rodin's iconic "Le Baiser" on the West Terrace, were the most acclaimed in Edna's photographs.

The exhibit was a great success and the biggest names in fashion design were mentioned with praise. All the photographs Edna made in that day were published in the fashion magazine, and Edna added many of them to her own collection. She asked Richard about the exhibit:

"How did you like it?"

"I've seen so many like this that there was nothing new to impress me; everything is all about big money. I must say though, that I liked a lot the photographs made by you in the Tuileries. They are indeed outstanding, and I'm immensely proud of you."

"Thank you, my love. I would like to go to the Louvre museum. How long it takes to see it?'

"Months, maybe years if you're an expert in art."

"Well, since I'm not an expert, my first choice would be *Mona Lisa*, and then Vermeer's *The Lacemaker*, and Veronese's *The Wedding Feast at Cana*."

"I'll book the tickets and we'll go next week. After that we'll go to the Philarmonie de Paris Concert Hall to listen some music. What do you say?"

"I love when you plan something that we both like to do."

The visit to the Louvre was a great reward for both of them. The halls were quite crowded, but the spectators spoke in whispers, moving from one painting to another. It was a general atmosphere as in a holy place where people are in silent prayers. In front of the painting of Mona Lisa, there were no words to say but only to show respect and admiration without limits. The painting was in a sealed glass enclosure and the audience could only get as close as it was permitted.

Turning to Vermeer's work, Edna could not hide her excitement for the amazing technique used by the artist. The composition as well as the color accents emotionally impress the spectator who is absorbed by the combination of reality with the imagination outlined by the young embroiderer.

"It's amazing how much it accentuates the feelings that overwhelmed him when he painted it", she said.

They went forward to see Veronese's *Wedding Feast at Cana,* which combines the Venetian colors of Titian with design of the High Renaissance representing the varied means of expression and various advances in painting technique. The work symbolizes the interplay between earthly pleasure and earthly mortality with breathtaking details, expressing allegorical and symbolic features.

On that day, they stayed until closing time and saw some pieces of art from different eras, of amazing artistic beauty.

"You didn't tell me what your preferences were," Edna said.

"Any piece that inspires me deep feelings and artistic mastery."

"Next time I would like to see the collection of Impressionists and Post-Impressionists."

"For this we have to visit the Musée d'Orsay which is famous for the world's largest collection of Impressionist and Post-Impressionist paintings. It is a smaller building, but with an interesting history. The original structure was a railroad terminal called *Orléans station,* built in the late 19th century. As stated by descriptions, the architecture is beautiful and the building itself is worth seeing.

According to historical information, Vincent van Gogh produced almost thirty self-portraits because he wanted to practice painting faces. One of them is at the Musée d'Orsay."

"How do you know so much about Paris?"

"I read."

The Musée d'Orsay was indeed at the level described in the art albums. The five-story building was an architectural masterpiece, and the collection of paintings exceeded two thousand exhibits. Edna took a lot of photos, especially details, just like she did at the Louvre. She was extremely pleased when after developing the films, they were ready to be studied from a closer approach.

"What is your style of painting?", Richard asked.

"I try to express the shades of color to fit not so much the subject, but my feelings which combine in a correct tonal value the reality I see with my imagination. In each brush stroke I invest my thoughts and my feelings, expecting the whole painting to become a portrayal that could reveal my personality."

"One day you'll be famous."

"I don't look for fame. I just do what I like the most and gives to my soul a feeling of plenitude."

"Would you like us to go next time to see the Eiffel Tower?"

"That's one place I don't like. It's gigantic, and completely out of the city's scale. Paris is renown for its long time history, its beauty, its arts, its architecture, and its elegance. The Tower has none of these, but became a symbol by stealing them and condensing them in the minds of foreigners so that they remember Paris through its image. If you want, you can go alone."

"No, I think you're right."

"I was thinking that I miss a lot working on my paintings. I need a room and I don't have one. Linette allows me to paint only on the balcony and that's not enough. I think that I have to do something about."

"I'll tell you exactly what we're going to do. We'll buy a house with many rooms and you'll have your studio to do your work. What do you say?"

"Sounds awesome, but can we afford to buy a house? It must be very expensive."

"Yes, we can, and we'll start looking tomorrow. I know a real estate agency and we'll have our house."

For the next days, the agent showed them a few houses, but none seemed right to them. After several other searches, he found a house in the suburb of Vésinet known for its wooded boulevards, mansions and lakes. Vésinet is located on a bend in the Seine, but has no access to the river and it's ten miles west of Paris, and four minutes to the subway. It was an exceptional residence at the end of the 19th century, combining character, harmony, and elegance, all exquisitely furnished including a standard size piano. It was very bright, and completely renovated with views of the garden and lawns. On the ground floor: large entrance hall, cloakroom, triple living room with fireplace, study, shower room, parquet floors, east-west crossing opening onto two terraces, fitted and equipped kitchen. On the 1st floor: four beautiful bedrooms with dressing room, bathed in light, and three large bathrooms. Basement had a multipurpose room, a laundry room, and the garage. Next to, it was a shed which could be used as storage. All around was a beautiful landscaped garden with trees and flowers with automatic watering, all fenced.

"How do you like it?", Richard asked.

"How are we going to pay?"

"We'll find a way. This is a marvelous house and I want us to have it."

"Have you lost your mind? We'll be evicted after a couple of months for not making the payments. We have a little savings which we keep for emergencies and we cannot touch it. We are hard working people and we are not rich to afford luxury. Don't you have a little common sense?"

"The agent promised a good deal so that we can afford to buy this house. Besides, our savings is not so small, and we can make the down payment."

"It's your call, Richard. Make sure that you know what you're up to."

The month of April came by, and it was Richard's birthday.

"What would you like for a gift?", Edna asked.

"I have everything that makes me the happiest man in the world. I want us to stay home and have a good time. I love you and Aden more than you can imagine."

"That makes my life easier. I love you both the same, and I must say that I'm happy too."

After a month, they moved into their house.

"With your permission, or without it, I will take the bedroom in the corner to make it my studio. It has plenty of light, and a big walk-in closet that will be a dark room. You two choose whichever you want from the three left, and start placing your things where they belong", Edna said.

The first thing Richard did was to take Aden in his lap and start playing at the piano Brahms' *Lullaby*. The baby felt a great pleasure, because he started making sounds and clapping his hands.

"Very well, my boy. Start learning and you'll become a pianist."

"He is not even seven months old, and you already make plans for his far future?"

"My dearest, he needs to exercise his hearing with harmonious sounds, and it's never too soon making plans for his future."

He took her hand and said with warmth in his voice:

"I missed this, my love. I missed my piano since I was young and never had a chance to play it again."

She kissed them both, saying:

"I'm happy that you can have it. I'm looking at you two thinking that I have everything in my life to cherish and care for. Aden is a miracle for us both. Look at him; he has my eyes and my hair, but inherited your traits, especially your smile."

He embraced them both with all the love of his heart.

In the meantime, Linette, examined every room and every corner of the house, unable to contain her admiration for everything she saw. Especially, the exquisite furniture, gave her a feeling of great pleasure and well-being.

"Unless you won the lottery, I don't see how you're going to pay for all these."

"Ask Richard; he has miraculous possibilities."

Over the next few days, Edna and Linette managed to organize the whole house by arranging everything in its place, while Richard was at work. They went shopping for food, and found the grocery store right around the corner of the street.

"The kitchen is large like to have a party there, but I don't even know how to use all those appliances", Linette said.

"We'll learn together, because I don't know either."

That week Edna and Richard went to the Opera House hosted in the Palais Garnier, to see Vincenzo Bellini's *Norma*. They were amazed by the splendor of the thirty-meter high vaulted architecture, built of marble of different colors. The horseshoe-shaped auditorium was designed so that the public could see and be seen. The ceiling repainted by Marc Chagall was shown as an allegory of winged characters, Parisian buildings and monuments. The entire hall was blinded by balconies in onyx, marble, and rich frescoes like never encountered in other artistic places in the world.

The music and the interprets were outstanding giving a spectacle ever to remember.

For the next days, Edna worked on her paintings, enjoying every single minute of it. She even skipped meals and Linette had to bring her a tray with whatever she cooked.

"I'll be very much obliged if you come to the dining room and behave like a civilized person. Also it would be nice if you cook from time to time, since I have to take care of Aden."

"Yes, you're right, Linette, but I have to work hard because I intend to open a gallery."

"When are you going to open it?"

"When I'll have the money, which I don't have now. I'm thinking, maybe I could give painting lessons, and make some money; they are very well paid."

Edna talked with Richard about the subject.

"I know how important is the gallery for you, but maybe you should wait a little and see how we can open it with only the money we have."

Edna had no time to wait for. She placed ads in art magazines and hoped that some amateurs will show up. In the meantime, she organized her studio to fit about four people and all the necessary equipment. After one week, two young men and one woman came to the house and enrolled in Edna's class. They were beginners, willing to learn the technique of oil and watercolor painting.

The weather was mild in that spring, and sometimes working outside on the lawn was a very good experience for them, especially in learning how to use mid-toned colors and to scale the subtle contrast between shades of light and shadow.

Three more applicants came to acquire knowledge from Edna's art skill. She scheduled them in a way that all could have the same coverage regarding the extent of learning.

In the meantime, when he came home from work, Richard helped Linette with the jobs around the house and the care for Aden. They both understood Edna's big efforts to make money for opening her gallery, and both gave her all the help she needed.

In fall, Edna could start looking for a location to open her gallery. She made enough money from teaching art during summer, and she could afford to make her dream come true. A few days later, Richard found a spacious two-room location just right for exhibiting Edna's work, on Rue Saint-Maur, which was about 30 minutes far from Place de la Concorde.

It took them a week to arrange about twenty-five paintings and forty photos, set out by subject in an order they considered most attractive. Edna made some announcements in art magazines, hoping that there would be at least a few amateurs visiting the exhibition. At the end of September, the gallery was opened and the first curious people began to appear, with a doubt at first, regarding the quality of the work displayed by an unknown name. In front of the exhibits, some were talking to each other, others were watching from a distance, and some stopped for a longer time in front of a subject that seemed to arouse their curiosity. From time to time, Edna was asked about the technique used or about the reason for choosing a subject, to which she gave precise answers and without showing intimidation. A few spectators were interested in buying some exhibits and the prices were advantageous; Edna did not expect a more generous offer. After two weeks, she managed to sell most of the paintings and photographs, making a considerable sum of money. In art magazines, articles praising the exhibits appeared, mentioning her remarkable art, especially of landscape photographs, which were so well made that they appeared almost like paintings. One of the reviews mentioned Edna's name with great appreciation as an unknown artist who "jumped out of nowhere to everywhere."

"What are your plans for the future? I'd like you to rest for a while", Richard said when they got home."

"I feel the need to be more with Aden and you. I have time to relax, and later I'll start working for the next exhibition. The money I've earned from lessons and from the gallery help us for a while to make payments for the house. I would also like to hire a housekeeper to come once a week and a gardener to come once a month. We need help to maintain the house and the lawn and we can pay them with ease. Linette will take care of finding and training them."

"I think it's a very good idea, especially now that you can't do the housework like before."

Linette was very happy to take on her new job.

"I'm pleased playing boss and being in charge of two employees."

"Enjoy it then," Richard said.

To celebrate the success of the gallery, they went to the Philharmonie de Paris to watch Brahms' *Symphony 1* and Rachmaninoff's *Piano Concerto No. 2*. The building was in a modern style completely different from the known classics. It was perched on a hill overlooking part of the city and had innovative spiral aluminum shapes surrounding the central concert hall. The balconies were connected with catwalks leading to the windows that connected to the foyers and other functions. The classical style was completely missing in the concert hall, with audience seating not only in front of the orchestra but also on the sides and behind.

Even if not pleased with that modern design, Edna and Richard enjoyed a lot the music and the performers.

Two days later, on October 2, Aden's birthday came and he was one year old. He was well developed for his age, could stand up, and even take a few steps. He could articulate a few words in a language mixed with French and English and recognized everyone around him. He called them "Mama" and "Dada" already, and for Linette he found the short word "Nette". Every time Richard played the piano, Aden became enthusiastic, made sounds of joy, and clapped his hands and feet.

"He seems to have musical talent, as does his father," Richard observed.

"Then you must cultivate it and make it work. I don't expect him to like painting as does his mother, but I hope he'll like music and maybe he'll be very good at it."

One evening, Edna received a phone call with a woman's voice saying that a friend bought two paintings from the gallery, and showed them to her. She liked the style in which Edna painted and decided to commission her to make her life-size portrait.

"My name is Madeleine Aubert, and if you are interested in my proposal, I will be waiting for you tomorrow morning at ten to discuss an arrangement. She gave her the address and Edna promised to meet her. Richard was not at all pleased:

"It was about resting and spending more time with family."

"Madame Aubert lives in Passy, which is the area of billionaires and the most powerful politicians. Do you know what that means, my dear? That means she pays a lot and makes me advertised to others just as rich. We need money, Richard, and this is a unique opportunity for us. I will not get tired, because I will convince her to work at home."

"I'm not happy at all, but I can't discourage you either. You have an appointment at ten when I have to be at work; I'll be late, but I'll drive you because Passy is far away. You'll be back by taking the subway."

The next morning, Edna took her camera and her briefcase, and they both left for Passy on the right bank of the Seine; they arrived at the address after forty minutes; Richard wished her success and went to work. Edna was in front of a grand villa with carved wooden door and stained glass windows. A butler dressed in the traditional code invited her into the hall, and then told her that Madame was waiting for her in the drawing room. Edna looked around and was amazed at the richness of the place; slowly, she followed the butler up the spiral staircase, which was very large and astonishingly elegant. On the walls were lined up paintings with various subjects, in different styles, and arranged according to the importance probably chosen by the owner of the house.

The drawing room was very large, and all the walls were covered with paintings. Madame Aubert was sitting in an armchair reading a magazine. She invited Edna to sit opposite her and without any introduction entered directly into the subject:

"I want you to make my life-size portrait in this dress. Tell me what your conditions are."

"I will first take photos and sketches, after which I will paint the portrait."

"You mean I won't have to pose for that?"

"Would you rather prefer to pose for four or five hours a day for two or three weeks?"

"Of course not, but I've never heard of such way of doing a painting."

"Let us be clear from the beginning, Madame Aubert. If you like the painting, you will keep it and pay me at the price you'll consider fair. If you don't like it, I'll keep it and you won't owe me anything. Agreed?"

"Yes, of course."

Edna took almost a hundred of photos from all corners and sides, telling her how to sit, how to move, how to talk, and how to smile. After that, she took sketches of her face, dress, body, and positions. She finished with everything in about five hours.

"We're done, Madame Aubert. I'll call you when the painting will be ready. Good day."

Madame Aubert was pleasantly surprised but also full of doubt.

Edna arrived home when it was already evening and Richard started to be worried.

"Did you eat anything today?"

"No. I'll eat tomorrow."

"I don't care about the money, if you get sick. I only care about you and Aden."

"Don't worry, I'll be fine."

Next morning, Edna developed the films and lined up the photos on the table. They looked very well done and she was pleased. Richard came from work and she asked him to take a look and tell her his opinion.

"They are very well done. This lady is attractive, although I can't say that she is beautiful."

"The pictures on the walls, you think they are originals or copies?"

"Can't say, unless I could examine them from a closer look. If only some are originals, she must be enormously wealthy. How long it will take you to make the painting?"

"Six weeks to two months, the least. I have to put multiple layers that need to dry and this takes several days for each. I wouldn't be able to work for the fall fashion line, since I have to concentrate on this one. It's a hard work especially since I've never been commissioned by someone to make a painting, and somehow I'm intimidated."

"Don't be. You're a great artist with remarkable talent. Besides, I'm always here to support you, no matter what the outcome will be."

She kissed him with all the love and trust of her soul.

Edna began work the next morning, promising Richard and Linette to take breaks and observe mealtimes. From time to time, she went to see her child and spend a few minutes with him, both enjoying each other's closeness. While in her studio, she was so concentrated on her work that mostly forgot about for how long she didn't move her body. Many times she didn't even notice that Richard or Linette opened the door and watched her in silence as she worked, then slowly retreated without making a whisper. Usually around seven in the evening was the time for her to finish for the day and join her family.

The painting was finished at the end of November after almost two months of hard work. Richard and Linette were both stunned with admiration.

"It needs a frame and here I'm asking you to help me, Richard."

"It fits a classic frame that we at the museum have a lot of. I'll ask the director to give me one for my wife who is a painter. I'm sure it will be possible to dispense with a frame that otherwise costs a lot.

Let's take the painting and frame it at the museum where there are all the necessary tools to make it have a laudatory presentation. Wait for me to bring the museum truck because the painting doesn't fit in our car. I'll be back in half an hour."

Richard hurried back and both went to the museum to frame the painting. The director had given his approval for the frame and expressed a desire to meet Edna. After the introductory formalities, he looked at the painting made by Edna and congratulated her, saying that he was impressed by the details and the tones of the colors, and that her talent would surely be highly recognized and appreciated in the artistic community.

"I know Madame Aubert very well. She is a patron of the arts and has quite a big collection from which several paintings are original. How did she find you?"

Edna told him about her gallery and how a friend of Madame Aubert who bought a couple of her paintings recommended her.

"She wouldn't have asked to paint her portrait if she had not noticed unusual talent in your work. I'll ask her for the painting to be displayed in the new section for the young contemporary artists, which I'll open in January. Also, if you have some paintings I'll be glad to exhibit them on the walls of the museum. What do you think?"

"I'll be honored Sir."

Congratulations again!"

They arrived at the exact time set for the appointment. The butler led them into the drawing-room, telling them to wait a few minutes for Madame. In the meantime, they unpacked the painting and leaned it against the wall that received light from the windows. Richard had just begun to examine the paintings on the walls, taking great pleasure in noticing their quality, when the door opened and Madame Aubert appeared in the room. An expression of astonishment appeared on her face when she saw the painting and she couldn't make a move. Without saying a word, she approached the painting, examining it in details from near and far. After a while, she exclaimed:

"Outstanding! It's amazing how you managed to render the delicate pastel shades of the voiles and how you painted the transparency in several layers of their finesse that intertwine with each other. It is also amazing how you rendered the expression of my face and the bright details of the dress embroidery. I'm very impressed by your remarkable skill and talent and I'm extremely pleased with the painting."

Then she noticed Richard and asked:

"Who might be you?"

"Her husband, Madame. It's a pleasure meeting you."

"Are you a painter also?"

"I'm curator of a museum."

She took a long look at him and then addressed Edna:

"Did you figured out the price for your work?"

"It is only up to your consideration."

Madame Aubert went to her desk, wrote the check and handed it to Edna:

"I hope this will be satisfactory".

Edna looked at the check and was stunned; she barely could whisper:

"Thank you for your generosity, Madame Aubert. We'll be going now. Good day."

On their way out, Edna was shaking when she showed Richard the check; he was amazed and had a short trembling when he said:

"It is ten times more than the painting is worth. We can make easy the payments of the house for at least three years, if not longer. My dearest, I really don't have the right words to say how I feel."

"No need. I feel stunned as you are, and I want us to go home and celebrate just talking and playing with our baby. I got tired lately and I need a break from work. The weather is starting to get cold and rainy; when you're not home, I'd like to walk with Aden on the meadow, play with him, and feel like I'm really resting. I read to him stories, talk to him a lot and he learned many new words that he remembers and recognizes. I want to make a few more paintings to open the gallery and that's what I think I can do."

"You have enough exhibits to open it but you are exhausted and I want you to rest first of all. We'll see later how and when we'll open the gallery."

A few days later, Edna received a phone call from Madame Aubert, saying that her best friend was excited seeing the portrait and wanted to commission her for a similar work. Edna replied that she has a project now; she is very busy, and later when she will be freer she will call her. Richard expressed his delight:

"If you gave her such an answer, it is the greatest proof to me that you are really exhausted and do not have the strength to work during this time. No matter how tempting the proposal is, there is no need to accept it for now, and it is good that you refused."

One morning Edna received a phone call with a woman's voice:

"My name is Mireille Dubois and I would appreciate a few minutes of your time for a personal issue that interests us both."

Edna looked surprised, especially when she detected a shake in the woman's voice. She thought for a moment what to answer and decided to accept the request for an appointment, but only after Richard will be back home from work; she replied that she could receive her around five o'clock and gave her the address. Edna told Richard about the incident, asking him if he knew the name of the woman who called.

"I haven't heard of her, but she's probably someone who wants you to make her portrait. We'll see what she wants and who she is."

At five o'clock, the person rang the doorbell and Edna opened it. In the doorway was a woman in her forties who kept silent without saying a word. Edna froze, and then shouted so loudly that Richard and Linette both appeared alarmed:

"Sister Agnes!! I can't believe it's you!"

"Edna, my dear little girl!"

They both jumped into each other's arms overwhelmed with a strong emotion that neither could control. Richard had to intervene:

"Come inside, and maybe you can tell me what's going on."

"Richard, this is Sister Agnes who raised me and I've told you so much about her! This is my husband Richard, and this is Linette, my baby's nanny."

"My name is now Mireille Dubois, and I'm very pleased to meet you both. Please call me Mireille."

They all sat down in the living room and Edna asked her to tell the whole story in the smallest details. Mireille wanted to see first the baby, and looked at him a few moments only, because Aden was asleep, but she mentioned how beautiful he was.

"After your disappearance, the convent became for me a deserted and empty place that I could no longer bear, and I understood that I no longer belonged there. I felt the need to leave it and return home to my family. It was very difficult for me until they let me go but in the end I succeeded and went to Vouvray, the place where I was born and raised; it's a pretty little town just east of Tours on the northern bank of the Loire. It was an emotional reunion when I saw my parents and sister again, who had no hope of ever seeing me again. I found a job as a teacher in kindergarten and I easily integrated into my new life in which I felt happy. Soon, I met Robert who had a small vineyard by the town, we fell in love with each other and got married; we have an eight-year-old girl, whom we adore. In your remembrance, we named her Alice as the little girl in your favorite story, who was protected by a fairy sent by an angel from heaven. You always said that I was like the fairy who protected you and you were sure that I was sent by an angel from heaven."

She showed them a lot of pictures, and continued:

"I thought often about you Edna, what might have happened to you, if you found the way you looked for, or if you were still alive; I was always worried about you. One day, by chance, I read in an art magazine, your name mentioned with admiration as being recognized in the artistic community as a great talent. I told myself that there could be no confusion and that it was definitely about my dear Edna. Then I talked to Robert and told him that I had decided to look for you and find you. I have no words to express how I feel and how happy I am to see you again. Now, tell me about yourself in few words, since it's getting late and I have to go home."

"Can't you stay with us overnight? I have so much to tell and share with you."

"I wish I could stay, my dear, but I don't want Robert and Alice to get worried; I promised to be back home by late evening."

"Let me talk to them, and I'll explain everything."

Mireille talked to her husband and put Edna on the phone who convinced him to let his wife stay overnight, without being worried.

Edna took a lot of pictures in that evening, promising to send them in the next few days.

During that night, Edna told the entire story since she left the convent, both talking a lot until it was almost morning.

It was time for Mireille to leave, and both Edna and Richard took her to the train station, promising that maybe in spring they'll come to visit her and her family at their vineyard in Vouvray. They all had a time to always treasure and never to forget.

"You know something?", Richard asked.

"Thrill me."

"I would very much like Debra and Glen to come visit us for Christmas and have a little vacation with us. What do you think?"

"This is wonderful, Richard, and I would like us to pay for their tickets. Until then, I'll prepare all the paintings and photos I already have, to reopen the gallery by the middle of December."

Edna's name was already well renowned, and this time, at the opening of her gallery, she dared to ask for quite high prices and obtained them easily, managing to sell almost all the exhibits.

A few days before Christmas, Debra and Glen arrived happy to see each other again after such a long time. They were received with much love, and all were eager to tell everything that happened in their lives, although they saw each other almost daily on the small screen and were well informed about each other. Most of all, they enjoyed keeping Aden by turn in their arms, who smiled and spoke in his language all the time. The weather outside was cold and the snow had begun, which prevented the possibility of visiting the city as they wished, but still, they managed to cover short distances and get a brief idea of the beauties they encountered.

When asked by Richard how they left the diner for the two weeks of vacation, Glen replied:

"With my nephew who is a man of great trust, so we have no worries. I want to benefit from every minute we are with you because it is not known when we will be able to see each other again."

They celebrated Christmas Eve with songs and ordered food, enjoying together that reunion, which everyone had been waiting for a long time. The adorned tree was the great pleasure of Aden who wanted to touch every ornament and colored light. Gifts were bought by Edna and Richard for each, producing great pleasure and joy in those times that proved to be valuable to all.

Debra and Linette became very friendly and had a lot of chats with topics that interested both of them. After Christmas, the weather became less cold, the snow stopped, and Glen and Debra expressed their desire to visit the Eiffel Tour. That day, Richard offered to please them, and they all left in the morning, except Edna, who stayed at home with Aden; anyway, she didn't like that scenic attraction. That day, Edna read stories to Aden showing him pictures from his book, just to teach him new words that he could understand and remember. They returned when it was almost evening, and each described the great pleasure they had, especially when they reached the highest top from which the whole of Paris was seen as a field of crowded houses.

As a special treat for them, the next evening they went to the Opera House to see Verdi's *Aida*. Debra and Glen were intimidated by the magnificent beauty of the auditorium hall, and they all were deeply impressed by the splendor of the spectacle.

They celebrated the New Year with even more feelings of closeness to each other, and Edna took a lot of photos that will remain as a memory of unforgettable moments.

A few days later, the new section of the museum was opened with exhibitions of young contemporary artists. Edna participated with four of her paintings, which were placed next to the portrait of Madame Aubert. Visitors crowded the hall, especially in front of the portrait painted by Edna, which seemed to have been the main attraction of the exhibition. Debra and Glen were enthusiastic about the presentation and especially about the paintings executed by Edna.

"Looks like you've become a celebrity," Edna heard a voice behind her.

It was Madame Aubert who admired the paintings, and she was accompanied by her friend.

"I'm Claire Bernard, who failed to commission you for my portrait. You're really very young but I found that you have a remarkable talent."

"Madame Aubert, thank you for your appreciation. Thank you, Madame Bernard, for your kindness. I will be honored to paint your portrait, and I hope to execute it with all my skill. At the moment I am caught up in some projects that I have to finish, but next month will be the most suitable, with your acceptance."

"Better later than never. I look forward to your proposal and let me know when you're ready to visit me; here is my business card. I must add that

I'm extremely impressed with your exhibits. Good day, and I'm waiting for you to call me."

Richard, Debra and Glen overheard the whole conversation, and were very pleased by the opinions of the two ladies. The director joined them and congratulated Edna:

"Your exhibits are the main attraction and they will bring a great appreciation of the new section from the art critics. Maybe one day, I'll commission you to paint my portrait; you never know", he said smiling.

After a few days, it was time for Debra and Glen to leave. The breakup was very sad even though they promised each other to be in constant contact.

In the beginning of March, Edna went to the address of Madame Bernard to start her portrait.

The house was as rich as Madame Aubert's, but with fewer paintings lined up on the walls.

The butler led her into the drawing room, where Madame Bernard was waiting for her, sitting in an armchair and holding a white, very neat poodle. She was extremely elegantly dressed, in a red and black ecossaise suit, high-heeled black shoes, and a red hat with large brim. She asked Edna a few professional questions and then decided together the most appropriate position for a life-size portrait.

"Do you want me to paint the poodle too?"

"She's Fifi, my baby, and yes, I want her to be in the painting."

Like she did before, Edna took almost a hundred photos and sketches, and after about four hours, she said:

"I'll be working on the portrait between four to six weeks, and I'll call you when I'm ready."

"Do you want a down payment?"

"No, Madame, there is no need. Good day."

Next morning, Edna developed the films and lined up the photos on the table next to the sketches she made.

"This one looks better than the other one; she is more attractive", Richard said. "Are you going to paint the dog too?"

"She's Fifi, and she's her baby, and yes, she'll be in the painting too."

They both had a big laugh and made some comments about rich people.

After five weeks of hard work, Edna finished the portrait and was very pleased with how it turned out. Richard expressed his opinion:

„It's awesome; she is extremely attractive, the expression in her eyes is intensely suggestive, and Fifi's eyes are admirably lively. You surpassed your talent with this painting and I'm sure Madame Bernard will be overwhelmed with its beauty."

"Thank you my love; your appreciation matters to me more than anyone else's and makes me believe in my artistic possibilities with much more élan."

The next day, they took the painting to Madame Bernard, who was waiting for them. At the sight of the portrait, first, she was speechless, then she began to analyze closely its details, making short sounds, and then she started jumping around and clapping.

"It's wonderfully beautiful! I'm amazed and thrilled! Finally, I have an admirable thing in this house to love and to be able to fully enjoy!"

Fifi began to bark, while Edna and Richard remained silent and stood at a considerable distance, looking at that woman who behaved like a child enjoying an expensive toy. Then she continued:

"For a long time or maybe never I had as much pleasure as I have now when I look at this portrait. Tell me how much I owe you."

"It is only up to your appreciation. The joy and pleasure you showed signify a great reward for me."

Madame Bernard smiled and went to her desk where she wrote the check, then handed it to Edna. At the sight of the number, Edna had a slight tremor, and she could barely control her emotion.

"Thank you for your generosity."

"You deserve it. Your talent is remarkable and certainly very rare."

"Thank you, Madame. Good day."

Going down the stairs, on the way to the car, Edna gave Richard the check and made him stop walking. The wonder he had was indescribable.

"It is much above than what Madame Aubert paid you, and she was extremely generous. This pay goes beyond any expectations and imagination I could have."

"She is extremely wealthy; she owns several very expensive buildings and hotels. I'm stunned, Richard. With this money we almost can pay the house, and have no more worries."

"Oh, dearest, I don't have words enough to say anything anymore. Let's go home and celebrate just being together with our baby. I want you to have a long rest and not working for a while."

A few days later, the painting was displayed in the museum alongside that of Madame Aubert's, and attracted a lot of visitors who expressed their enthusiasm. Overnight, Edna's name became famous and she became a celebrity. Critics in art magazines highly valued her talent, strongly asserting their opinion that she is one brilliant painter of the young generation.

After about one week, Madame Bernard called. Edna put the phone on the speaker, so that Richard could hear the conversation:

"I would like you to paint a mural on the wall of one of my elegant hotel. I have a dozen of friends who are eager to pose for you and would like to seek immortality through being painted on a mural by a famous artist like you."

"Thank you for the compliment Madame Bernard, but, sorry, I don't do murals. It will keep me away from my family for months."

"Madame Mathis, I'll pay you a fortune; you could buy a very expensive house even in Passy."

"With all due respect, you can pay me to buy the whole city, my answer will be the same. Besides, I have a house and I don't need to live in Passy."

"In case you change your mind, I'll be here, and you can call me at anytime. Goodbye for now."

"That's all we needed! This woman won't give up", Richard said. "Let's go for a small vacation, somewhere. How about if we go and visit Mireille, your friend who invited us to stay a few days with her and her family at their vineyard? Give her a call."

Mireille was delighted to see them and in the coming weekend, they all went to Vouvray which was about three hours of driving.

The Vouvray region is situated on top a plateau that is dissected by small streams and tributaries of the Loire; vineyards are usually planted on the plateau above the river bank. The town of the same name was quite small, with narrow streets and houses close to each other. In an elevated spot overlooking a valley of undulating green hills, the house of Dubois family made from stone and featuring decorative tile, had far-reaching views over a vineyard of about thirty acres. The garden was in the back of the house and was very well maintained.

The whole family received the newcomers with a lot of warmth and friendship, inviting them to the main room that served as a living room and as a reception room.

Robert came up with a proposal:

"Richard, you and I, we'll go to the wine cellar and taste the wine that was awarded last fall. You will also like the architecture of the cellar, which was built from a cave formed by the excavation of tuffeau rocks. At the same time, I think that the ladies have a lot to talk about and they will appreciate the time to be together. We'll meet at lunchtime. What do you think?"

Everyone agreed. After they left, Alice asked Edna's permission to take Aden to the garden where she could play with their puppy and there was plenty of space where they could both run. Linette agreed to join them, saying that she had to keep an eye on him because he was playful and had to be watched. Remaining both, Mireille and Edna had much to tell each other from the past and from the recent times.

"I want to show you something that might bring us both some nostalgic moments", Mireille said.

She took from the library a volume that looked familiar to Edna.

"This is one of my sketchbooks that I left behind because it didn't fit in my backpack!"

"You want it?"

"Oh, no. I want you to keep it. Here, are precious moments that we've spent together and were dear to us both. Wait a minute! There are some blank pages and I'm going to sketch you all to keep like a remembrance of our reunion after a long time!"

"When you disappeared, I was devastated, Edna. You were like my own child who was taken from me by an unjust fate. Maybe, that's why I became determined to leave the convent, and as you can see, it turned out that I made the right decision."

At noon, everyone returned, each happy with what had happened. Alice was excited about Aden's personality, who never got tired of playing with the puppy and running through the garden one after the other.

"He has a rich vocabulary for his age, and he likes to talk all the time even though some words aren't very clear, but probably because you speak to him in English and French and he kind of confuses them sometimes. He's an adorable kid! I wish I had a brother like him!"

Robert and Richard continued to discuss the problems of winemaking and they both showed that they had a wonderful time together.

After lunch, they all were tired and had a good nap until late afternoon. Till late evening, Edna sketched them all separately and in-group, and signed every drawing. It was a precious time for each of them to always be remembered.

After a few days, it was time to break up. They said goodbye to each other, making promises to see each other again and even to spend longer holidays together. They left later, and the way back seemed longer to them than on arrival; every one competed to tell about the wonderful time spent and the pleasure that each had in those few days of vacation; when they got home it was almost evening and everyone was tired. When alone, Richard asked Edna:

"May I ask you something that might be a sensitive subject for you?"

"Ask anything."

"I've thought many times, if you forgave your mother because she left you and never took an interest in you."

"I will tell you something Richard, which is part of my faith that I have established over the years by learning and understanding the realities of life. Forgiveness is a noble value of the human soul and is necessary in human relationships. However, it cannot be considered as an absolute measure that erases the mistakes made. Everyone has a consciousness that never lies, and only everyone can forgive himself or not, depending on how one thinks and feels. As for a mother and her child, there is an indestructible bond between them, established by the supreme law of Creation, and which dictates their lives regardless of their relationship. Mistakes made between them cannot be taken into account because they cannot be judged on a plan that does not actually exist for them. No matter how much a mother makes a mistake against her child or no matter how much a child makes a mistake against his mother, the bond between them remains the same and no one and nothing can ever destroy it. If my mother was a prostitute and I was born as a biological accident, or if she was raped and I am the product of that crime, or I was born for any other reason, it makes no difference between my connection with her. The issue of forgiveness or condemnation for what determined her to proceed with me in the way she chose is not even remotely raised. Is this answering to your question?"

"I love you and I love everything about you more than you can ever imagine."

"Hold me tightly, so that I can feel safe and nothing bad could happen to me."

Time went by, Aden was already four years old, and he had to be enrolled in preschool.

"You think that he needs that?", Richard asked.

"Yes, he does. He has to interact with other children and adults, he has to learn to share, socialize, and contribute to circle time. In preschool, he will develop social skills, work together with children, take turns, participate in-group activities, and follow directions. The program is three days a week, and three hours daily. I already took all information and I think is very good for him to attend preschool, before kindergarten."

"I don't know how you manage to make always everything right."

Aden loved the program from the first day, and he was enthusiastic about his classmates and the teacher. When he came home, no one could stop him from talking about everything that made him immensely happy.

One day, Linette told them the bad news:

"My daughter, Martine, divorced her husband and asked me to come live with her and her son. It is extremely painful for me to leave you, who are my family that I treasure, but I have to do the right thing and join my real family who needs me and I have to help."

Edna and Richard were awfully sad and Aden started crying, even he didn't understand other than his beloved Nette had to go and he might not see her again.

After Linette's departure, Edna took full charge of Aden's activities, while Richard did the best he could to help her. Both were determined to give him the best education a child could have, by increasing his desire to learn new meanings, enjoy everything he learned, and never get bored. For the time being, Edna gave up painting, while Richard encouraged him to listen to music, memorize short pieces, and try his musical skill on piano keys. After a while, Aden could read and play the notes quite well, besides being able to read stories from his books and write short sentences describing the characters. Quite often, they went to the concert hall, giving Aden the opportunity to watch a soloist playing with the orchestra, to listen, and get accustomed to the classical music.

Aden's personality gradually developed, asserting itself on a robust level of self-confidence and the desire to learn new things, which he then discussed with his parents. Gradually, the preschool program started to bore him and he was no longer interested in it. Every weekend, he talked to Linette on the small screen, telling her everything that had happened that week and always mentioning how much he missed her. Sometimes he played for her a piece of piano music; he enjoyed a great pleasure every time he learned something new, being instructed by Richard who could not hide his pride in seeing the progress his son was making. He acquired quite a considerable musical repertoire and was very earnest regarding his daily practice. One day, Richard told him:

"I'll play Debussy's *Clair de Lune* with intentionally a false note. You listen carefully and stop me when you hear it and tell me which note was wrong."

Richard started playing and after two minutes Aden shouted:

"Stop right there! You played *Sol sharp* instead of *Sol natural!*"

"Right, my boy! You are the pride of my life! Maybe soon, you're going on the big stage to compete in domestic and international piano competitions for best performance."

At the age of six, Edna enrolled him in first grade, thinking that eliminating the kindergarten phase would be a boon for him. It was a new atmosphere for Aden in which discipline was mandatory, meaning that was much to his liking because the lessons taught by his teacher could be listened without interruption. Only two weeks later, the school principal called his parents, telling them:

"Aden has a level of knowledge far above his classmates even though he is younger than them. Sometimes he is like absent from class, other times he finds something to do, or reads a book. I examined him carefully with his teacher, and we concluded that it would be much in his favor and in that of the school if Aden would be transferred to the third grade, where his level of knowledge is very suitable. I have called you so that together we can take this decision, if of course you agree."

Both Edna and Richard suspected that their son would not be satisfied with the beginners' curriculum, and would react in an unpleasant way that would upset the school management. At the principal's suggestion, they both agreed, hoping that the more advanced lessons would please Aden and he would behave according to his obligations.

Aden was delighted with that promotion, and in the same time, the school principal was pleased with the decision he made about that very young boy who seemed to have found his right place.

For several days, Edna noticed that Richard was preoccupied with thoughts that seemed to bother him and that he was looking for a solution to solve a difficult issue. She waited a while for him to tell her what problem he had in order to help him, but it seemed that he wanted to solve it himself, until she lost her patience:

"Talk to me, Richard."

"I don't want to bother you and that's why I'm trying to find a solution to a problem that has been bothering me for a while."

"I' m always by your side, whatever problem you may have. Talk to me."

"I thought about changing my occupation as a curator at the museum, and finding something more fulfilling to do. I'm very bored to move paintings from place to place, to negotiate new exhibits, and to answer visitors' questions. In addition to my master's degree in fine arts, I have the equivalent of a master's degree from the conservatory; I thought I could find a piano teacher position that would make me very happy, because classical music is a passion for me. I'm not sure if it's good to make this move or not about the job."

"What are you waiting for? No more time to think. Put your resignation paper on tomorrow, and immediately start looking for a position at the conservatory."

"I have more confidence in your reasoning than in mine. So I will."

For two weeks, Richard played piano from dawn to dusk, until he decided to make an appointment for a teacher position at the conservatory.

"You think he will get it?", Aden asked his mother.

"I only can hope; you tell me, you're the expert."

"I think he'll be a great teacher. He plays with feelings and knows a lot about music."

Next week, Richard went to the appointment, and found out that he will be tested by the director, joined by two members of the faculty and a musician from outside the conservatory. After about three hours, he was told that they'll make their decision in a couple of days and they'll call him.

In those two days, he was nervous all the time, pacing the room back and forth, and barely talking. Finally, he was called, and went to find out the decision taken by the commission.

The director started from the beginning:

"Your way of playing is impressive, and we decided to give you the job. Since you don't have any experience in teaching, you are qualified for the level of bachelor's program, which is the 1st cycle of undergraduate. However, you have a master's degree and you proved a great skill in playing music; therefore, the commission decided to make an exception, and give you the position of teacher in the master's program which is the 2nd cycle in our conservatory. Welcome to the faculty, Professor Werner. You'll start next week and congratulations for your success."

Richard was about to explode of so much happiness. He rushed home, and before saying anything, he took both, Edna and Aden in his arms, starting to dance and doing pirouettes. Only after he calmed down, he told them everything that happened at the interview. They both joined him showing their big enthusiasm, competing in expressing their happiness.

For the first time, Richard felt he had a fulfillment in his life in terms of the satisfaction of a career that had always been his desire to have it. From the first moment, a connection developed between him and the four students who were in his class and who from the beginning appreciated the high level at which their young teacher prepared them to become concert pianists. The following month, Richard came home with news that might have interested Edna and especially Aden:

"After two weeks, the conservatory's management will hold a party for one of the professors who is retiring after thirty years, and faculty members are invited with their families; some students will play music on different instruments. Aden, would you like to participate with one of the songs you know better?"

"Why not? I love to."

"Very good. Choose a piece of music, and start practicing until then. I will be by your side at every step and I would like you to present yourself at the highest level of your talent, with confidence and with a thorough knowledge of the details of the music you choose. We have a large audio and video music library with the most renowned performers; you can consult anytime the piece you like, and learn a lot while you play and practice."

Starting the next day, Aden devoted his time to playing Chopin's *Etude Op. 10 No. 3* and Beethoven's *Moonlight Sonata*. It was the first month of summer vacation, so he could focus exclusively on practicing music. Richard followed his progress, but always interrupted him by showing him misinterpretations, and forced him to repeat whole sentences.

"No, no, and no! Start again! Put some feeling in those fingers of yours!"

Aden showed signs of fatigue, and one day he exploded:

"I have enough! I don't want to play anymore, not for your conservatory experts, not for you, not for the whole world! Leave me alone!"

He dropped the notes on the floor and ran to his room. Edna approached Richard:

"Why do you put so much pressure on him? Do you forget he's barely seven? This way you will only make him move away from the pleasure of learning and performing music."

"I want him to live up to the extraordinary talent he has, and which must be cultivated carefully. I want him to be higher than any other musician in his generation; that's why I insist so much for him to learn the depth and finesse of classical music. Or rather, you want him to end up playing piano in a bar for drunken customers?"

"Or more precisely, you want to satisfy your ego and pride that were not realized in you because you did not have the opportunity to develop them; now, you want to prove your desires fulfilled by your son's piano interpretation with exemplary mastery of classical music. If he is under constant pressure, I don't care how he plays the piano, or what he will do later; he is my son whom I adore, and I give my life for him if I have to. Think carefully about what you want to do, Richard, so that you won't regret it later."

Edna went straight to Aden's room. He was lying on the bed with his eyes closed. She approached him and whispered:

"Let's go for a walk in the park, for a bit of exercise and fresh air. How would you like that?"

"Are you going to lecture me and tell me how to behave?"

"Not at all. If you want, we don't have to talk, but just walk and look at the people in the park."

"Then let's go."

It was a pleasant morning, with warm weather, sun, and clear skies. In the park, people sat on benches, talking and looking at the children playing on the lawn. Edna and Aden also sat on a bench in the shade, keeping quiet and watching only what the others were doing.

"It's very pleasant here," Aden opened the conversation. "I'm glad I came and I can have peace, away from music and piano."

"Do you enjoy learning new songs?"

"Yes, I like piano and music, if that's what you want to know, but I don't like it when Dad pisses me off over and over again when he thinks I'm wrong. I know I have to correct myself and he knows better how to play, but then I get tired and I feel like giving up music and piano altogether."

"Do you want me to tell you something about me that you probably don't know, and maybe you would be interested?"

"I want."

"Unlike your father who has a high music education, I have no education at all in this regard, because I did not have the opportunity in childhood and youth to be in contact with music. I first listened to music when I met your father who introduced me to opera and concerts. I don't know how to read notes and I don't recognize one note over another, but I really like listening to music, because it gives me a feeling that it fills my soul with a kind of richness of unique value. I feel warmth and delight as nothing else can give me more pleasure. You started listening to music since you were born and over the years, you started to like it more and more as you managed to enrich your musical knowledge and develop your talent. Of course, there is a big difference between a musician, as you will become, and a simple listener like me. A professional musician knows every note and every nuance of the piece he performs, being careful not to make mistakes and especially to respect the interpretation that the composer thought when he wrote it. Let me tell you what I think about this. Any piece of music is addressed to all listeners, regardless of the lack or degree of musical culture of each. I believe that for a great composer all that is more important is the way his composition is listened by the public, and not the criticism that music experts attribute to his composition. A music performer should think the same. The way he expresses his musical talent and education must include the feelings he experiences when he performs the musical song, and those feelings of his must be addressed to those who listen. Music is similar to painting. The colors have different shades that the painter expresses as he feels what is appropriate to the subject; the chosen shades are transmitted to the viewer who interprets the painting through the deep or superficial feelings expressed by the painter and which are absorbed by the mind of the viewer at the same level of intensity. If the painter fails to radiate the shades of colors that express his feelings, the viewer interprets the painting only through contour and shapes, in which the expression of colors becomes only a transient effect, leaving no emotions behind. As in painting, music has nuances of expression that the performer reveals by conveying the feelings that surround his soul with emotions when addressing his listeners. The nuances felt by the performer are assimilated by those who hear them, and their intensity or superficiality becomes an emotional source or remains a simple auditory experience. Music was composed for those who listen to it, who value it for the benefits it brings to the soul, and not for those who criticize it. If you want a friendly advice, when you play a piano piece of music, don't think about every note for fear of making a mistake; don't think of music experts who will criticize your performance, but only think of those like me whom to address yourself, with the conviction that you will be applauded in their souls and you will have the greatest satisfaction in your profession. Most of all, when you play music, think that you're alone only with your feelings, and you play it for yourself."

"I love you, Mom, for everything you just told me, and I understood very well every single word you said. You made me feel much, much better, now."

"I love you Aden for everything you are, and I'm happy that we understand so well each other."

When about to leave, a little boy approached and asked:

"Would you like to play soccer with us?"

"Yes, I'll be happy, and thank you for asking."

In short than few minutes, Aden mingled with the other children, while Edna kept looking at him, thinking that indeed, her son was her life.

They went home when Richard started already being worried.

"Where have you been all day? It's almost evening and you left before noon."

"We had a great time in the park. I played soccer!"

"Maybe you'll be a better soccer player than a piano player!"

"Maybe. At least I'll be good at something!"

"Stop it, both of you! Aden go take a shower, and I'll make dinner; don't be late."

"No plans for me?"

"Use your wisdom, Richard, it might help us all."

Over dinner, none of them spoke and the atmosphere was tense. Edna started doing the dishes; Richard sat on the couch reading a book, and Aden looked like he couldn't find his place. Suddenly, he went to the piano and started playing Beethoven's *Moonlight Sonata*. Both Edna and Richard became like electrified. He played with so much deep feelings that the music became like pouring from his soul. When he finished, he took a moment of silence and was ready to go to his room.

"I'm deeply impressed! It's wonderful! When did you learn to play like that?"

"Today, in the park. Good night."

"What miracle happened to him? He played totally different than before."

"Maybe he learned from the soccer game!"

The following week, Aden focused on the pieces of music he had chosen to play at the conservatory's party. Only sometimes did Richard interrupt him for minor, almost unobservable mistakes, which made them both understand each other better. On Sunday afternoon, the three of them went to the party, dressed like for a gala. The hall was arranged for at least fifty guests who were each seated around tables with each one's name on the plate. The director made the introduction mentioning the importance of that social gathering, followed by speeches honoring the retiring professor. After finishing the snacks and the clash of champagne glasses, a few students walked on stage and performed musical pieces on various instruments. The audience was delighted by their excellent performances and the applauses followed with great warmth for those young people who did their best to honor a professor admired and loved by all his students. It was already evening, when the audience became tired and everyone wanted to go home faster, when the director went on stage and announced:

"As a compliment to the success of our gathering, we will have the pleasure of listening to the youngest pianist tonight, who will demonstrate his ability as a musician at a very young age. Ladies and gentlemen, I present to you Aden Mathis Werner."

There were whispers of discontent in the audience, people being already tired and bored. Aden bowed to the audience and took his place at the piano after an assistant lifted his bench and brought the pedal extender. He had chosen to perform Beethoven's *Moonlight sonata* for that evening. After the first chords, there was a complete silence in the hall, and everyone's attention turned to that little performer who seemed to have a miracle in his fingers. Aden gave a completely exceptional performance; when he finished, there was a moment of silence, after which the whole audience rose to a standing applause. Aden bowed, thanking everyone, and left the scene. The applause continued to demand 'encore'. After his third appearance on the stage, Aden sat down at the piano again and performed Schumann's *Kinderszenen*. The success was huge, the applause was stormy, and everyone was trying to get closer to that boy who seemed to have been the main attraction that night. One of the professors asked him:

"Where did you learn to play so well?"

"I learned to play piano from my father and I learned to play music from my mother."

Both Richard and Edna hugged him with warmth and tears they could not control.

None of them found the right words to show the enthusiasm that overwhelmed all three and only on the way home, Richard managed to control his emotions and said:

"I must say that you played above my expectancies and I'm extremely impressed by your performance. I don't know what happened that day in the park and certainly, I'll never know, but since that day, you play the piano totally different from before. What I can be sure of is that between you and your mother is a strong bond that cannot be broken, no one in the world can touch, and I respect that even if I cannot ever be part of it. What I'm also sure of is that I love you both more than my life, and I'll be always there for you whether you need me or not."

"I love you, Dad, and I'm proud to be your son."

"I love you, Richard, and I'm happy to be your wife. I'm also there for you two, whether you need me or not. Now, let's relax and have a good time by exchanging our impressions from the party."

They talked, laughed, and joked till late night when all three felt exhausted.

A few days later, Richard came up with a proposal:

"Next month, the conservatory will hold a competition to promote young talents. Especially teenagers who intend to pursue musical careers will participate. The director asked me if you would like to participate, even though you are at a much younger age than the other competitors are. Would you be interested in competing?"

"Very much. I'm not scared at all of my age or that of others. Even if I don't manage to be in the first place, it will be an experience for me that will be of use to me as an exhibition in front of the public.

"I am very happy with your attitude. Which composition would you like to compete with? "

"I wanted to try Chopin's *Heroic Polonaise* for a long time. I will practice every day until then if you would like to help me."

"With all my heart and all my knowledge, but don't you think that a lighter piece that you know already would be more suitable for your first contest?"

"I want to try my potential and see what I can do without being afraid of failure. Please play the whole piece for me now, and I will follow the notes while you perform."

From that day on, Aden sat at the piano for hours, showing no signs of fatigue; it seemed that his progress made him very happy. Richard corrected him from time to time, but he too was especially pleased with his son's ambition to succeed. Meantime, Edna watched them both, thinking that they lived in a world of their own, where father and son built together a strong bond between them.

On the day of the competition, Aden was scheduled to play the last of the twelve candidates. The auditorium was composed mostly of the candidates' parents; in the first row of the seats was the jury made up of professors from the conservatory.

When Aden's turn came, his face showed the determination to present himself at the highest level he could reach. He gave indeed an excellent performance awarded with the second prize, which was a remarkable record for that level of competition, especially at his very young age.

The years went by, Aden become a tall, strong, and very handsome teenager. He graduated from high school at the age of fifteen and enrolled in the first cycle, equivalent to Bachelor's program, at the Conservatoire de Paris. The entrance exam was extremely difficult and out of thirty candidates only five were admitted, of which Aden was the youngest. In the past years, he had managed to accumulate an impressively rich musical repertoire, which he performed with great ease and competence. He was already known in the academic body of the conservatory as being exceptionally talented and well prepared for his career as a concert pianist.

"How do you like your teacher?", Richard asked.

"Not much, but she is all right."

"Meaning what?"

"Meaning that I would like to learn more than I already know, and she is not giving me what I need."

One day, Aden was called by the director who told him without any introduction:

"The director of the Strasbourg Conservatory has asked two pianist students to take part in a competition together with two of their students to perform Tchaikovsky's *Piano concerto No.1*. The winner will be sent to Vienna next year where he will play the concert with the symphony orchestra. The faculty of our conservatory has decided to send you and another student from the 2nd cycle. Would you like to participate in the contest? "

"Thank you for the trust you place in me, and I will do my best to live up to your expectations."

"You have three weeks to prepare."

Aden was overwhelmed with excitement when he broke the news to Richard and Edna.

"It will be the first time I'll play with the orchestra, and I have the ambition to succeed. It will be an experience I have never encountered before, and I have enough time to prepare."

Richard and Edna were very excited, both expressing their assurance that they will be with him at all times. From that day on, Aden sat at the piano most of the day practicing the concert under the supervision of Richard, who made the necessary remarks and made him repeat the musical phases that Aden felt insecure with.

After three weeks, they left in the morning by car for Strasbourg, a city in eastern France, where the Rhine forms the border with Germany. It was the beginning of October, and Aden's birthday, when he turned sixteen. After a five-hour drive, they arrived at the hotel, and Aden went straight to the conservatory to get all the information about the contest. He was told that the competition would start after two days, would take place in the evening, would last four days, and his name was last on the list of competitors, he being the youngest. Until the day of the competition, they visited the city where the main attraction is the more than twenty bridges with remarkable architecture. Also, the place where Mozart was hosted, during his last stay in Strasbourg, when he gave three piano concert performances.

The first night of competition was a success for the candidate of the local conservatory who opened the competition but seemed very nervous. In the first row of seats was the jury made up of music professors from the conservatory and musicians from outside with a recognized reputation in the country and abroad. All the time, they took notes of every movement of the competitor. In the following evenings, the candidates presented themselves acceptably, and the audience in the hall seemed satisfied with the performances of those young people who at their age had enough courage to perform a difficult concert in which the musician's expertise was welcome. Aden asked Richard and Edna to sit not far from him when he performs. That evening, he took his place in front of the piano, and at the signal of the conductor, he showed from the beginning full confidence and no sign of hesitation. He performed the whole concerto with great skill, without any mistakes, and the success was unexpectedly great.

After three days, Aden was told that he won the competition and he will perform next year the concerto with the Vienna Philharmonic.

Back home, Edna asked:

"How would you like to celebrate your birthday and your success in the same time?"

"In a very special way. I met a girl whom I like and she likes me too. I would like you both to meet her."

"That is a special way, indeed, and I'm impressed. Bring her home any time to meet her. Can you tell us a little bit of her background?"

"Her name is Carole Benoit, she is a student in the harp class, and she is very smart and pretty. Her mother died when she was three, and her father who is a pediatrician, remarried and they have a five years daughter, Denise who is cute and well mannered. Her stepmother is a nurse and they have a good relationship in the family. They both encouraged Carole to learn harp since she liked classical music and had the desire to learn that instrument at the level of conservatory. We both have a lot in common, even many features of our personalities, and we understand very well each other. I told you about everything, and I would like you both to meet her."

"Very interesting", Richard said. What took you so long to tell us?"

"I had to do my homework first, and see if we were compatible. Then, I had to find out about her family, and according to the book of etiquette, the girl introduces first the boy to her parents."

"It looks like you covered all the grounds. Bring her home any time you want. I'm sure we'll like her", Edna said.

Next day, Aden came with his girl. She was very well dressed, slender, graceful, and shy. A combination of brown hair with blue eyes, small nose, a beautiful smile, and fair complexion, made her very attractive and very pretty.

From the beginning, Edna and Richard liked her, and thought that Aden made a wonderful choice. The conversation started with few casual words, and it was quite tense, each one trying to make a good impression. During dinner, everyone felt more relaxed and the conversation entered a pleasant and interesting atmosphere. They talked about music, a performer's career, and the prospects for a bright future.

"I was kind of intimidated at first when Aden invited me to meet his parents, knowing the great reputation you both have; but I saw that I was received very warmly, and you did everything to make me feel comfortable. My relationship with Aden means a lot to me, because from the beginning I understood that we have many personality traits and feelings in common, and a similar way of thinking. Today, I also understood that I'm received in his family with kindness, and that means for me a great encouragement in the relationship between me and Aden. Thank you both very much for the kindness and warmth you showed me from the beginning."

Edna answered with emotion in her voice:

"It is a great pleasure for us to meet you, Carole, and we are very happy for our son who appreciates you so much and gave us the opportunity to know his feelings for you."

Soon, Carole became a regular of the family, coming often and always being received with great warmth by Edna and Richard. It was obvious that both Carole and Aden loved each other a lot and had become like a couple who built a strong bond between them.

"We plan to get married when we finish school and have a job," Aden said.

"We will bless that event and of course you will live with us."

"Thanks, Mom, you can be sure of that."

Christmas was near, and it was time for both families to get to know each other.

Carole was thrilled when Edna asked her to invite her family to attend the Christmas Eve dinner. That evening, the Benoit family, Jean, Emille, and Denise, appeared at the door, all carrying gifts and every one expressing great joy for the opportunity to meet. The couple was extremely pleasant and friendly, while little Denise was adorable indeed. It was an extremely enjoyable evening, with a lot of conversation, jokes, songs, and wishes of goodwill, prosperity, and lasting friendship on both sides. Near the decorated and lighted tree, they opened the gifts brought by the Benoits, and those prepared for them by Edna, Richard, and Aden. They broke up late, when little Denise was already asleep in the armchair; they decided to celebrate the New Year's Eve at the Benoits' house, hoping for a wonderful time, the same as in that evening.

In April, Aden was to leave for Vienna to perform Tchaikovsky's *Piano concerto No.1*. A week before, the three of them and Carole, boarded the plane and arrived after two hours at their destination in the evening. Before the concert there were two rehearsals with audience, at which Aden proved an excellent collaboration with the conductor and orchestra, considering that it was the first time he performed a piece of music accompanied by a prestigious philharmonic orchestra conducted by a conductor with a well-known reputation. On the evening of the concert, the opening was made with Mozart's *Symphony No. 35*, extremely well performed by the orchestra and much appreciated by the public. Aden followed, who seemed to be very confident, and from the first chords attracted the attention of the audience. The performance he executed that evening was completely exceptional, followed by vigorous applause from public and orchestra's members, and congratulations from the conductor.

"You're my hero", Carole said, and kissed him with all the love of her soul.

Richard showed big emotion when he said:

"I'm overwhelmed and extremely proud of you. The performance you gave us this evening surpasses all my expectancies."

Edna had tears in her eyes, didn't say a word, only embraced him, and cried when she mentioned that he gave her the biggest happiness since he was born. She managed to ask with a faint voice:

"How would you like to celebrate your success?"

"Ask me tomorrow Mom. Now it's late, I'm tired, want to relax and have a good night sleep."

The next day, all the newspapers described the marvelous success of that young pianist who conquered the hearts of the Viennese with his brilliant performance.

They stayed a few more days to visit the most sought after places by tourists.

"What languages are spoken here?" Aden asked.

"German first; although almost the entire population speaks English, but very little French, my knowledge of German would be very helpful, especially when it comes to services; we will manage very easily ", Richard replied. "Let's go to Stephansplatz first, which is the city's main square."

In that place rises the great Roman Catholic cathedral, Stephansdom, which is said to be one of the most beautiful Gothic structures in the world. Inside, the tall nave is decorated with baroque overlays, and the stained glass windows attract attention by the beauty of the details and drawings on display.

The next day, they visited the Schönbrunn Palace which has 1,400 rooms, of which 40 can be seen, complemented by the original decor and furniture. The royal apartments were of unimaginable richness and the galleries adorned with frescoes surpassed in splendor the most daring artistic expectations. All four were enthusiastic about the architecture and art of those places, recognized in history as representative of some of the most valuable artistic treasures.

The next evening they went to the State Opera, which dates from 1860 and retains the same grandeur from then. The entrance hall is elegantly decorated with frescoes, and the auditorium is built in such a way as to allow a complete view of the stage from any angle. That evening was the presentation of Gustave Charpentier's *Louise* in which the performers excelled, giving the music and the composer the appreciation they deserved. The aria *Depuis le jour* made Carole cry and shiver. Aden took her hand and whispered:

"Let this be our song."

"Yes, this is our song."

On the last night of their stay in Vienna, they celebrated Aden's success at the most luxurious restaurant, with music and dancing until after midnight.

In June, Aden and Carole graduated from first cycle of the conservatory equivalent to a bachelor's degree, and enrolled in the next cycle for the master's diploma. In the period that followed, they had both reached the degree of excellence in music education and performance. After graduation, Carole obtained the position of harpist in the Paris Philharmonic, and Aden enrolled in the third cycle of the Conservatoire for the doctoral program, which was the study of the composition of classical music.

The best time had come for them both to get married. They had a joined family celebration with a few colleagues only, and that was a great happiness for everyone; for their parents it was an emotional event, considering that the time had come when their children were ready to start their own family. They all decided that the newlyweds should live with Edna and Richard, and have at their disposal all the necessary comfort for everything they wanted to achieve.

In a short time, Aden and Carole proved to be an ideal couple who adored each other expressing their happiness in every moment of their lives. Carole had become very attached to Edna and Richard, who appreciated her behavior and personality, and were happy for the way she always revealed her affection for them. During the day, only Edna stayed at home, and they saw each other in the evening when the four of them met, each telling in details about how they spent their time. Often after dinner, Aden or Carole gave a musical performance, he on the piano and she on the harp, creating a warm atmosphere in which love radiated between them all.

From time to time, Aden was invited to give a concert, in various European cities with famous philharmonics, and left alone for a few days, after which he returned home full of success and gratitude. In those days, everyone in the family was worried not because he might have failed, but only because those roads he made, especially by plane, caused them anxiety and fear of an accident. Aden always smiled, assuring them that something unpleasant could never happen to him, but he never could convince them. Now and then, Richard or Carole, or both accompanied him, while Edna was left alone home, since she had to work on paintings commissioned by various personalities who paid high prices. In those days, she was worried all the time, even if she was in contact with her family, who tried to assure her that they were all right.

One day, at dinnertime, Carole made a big announcement:

"I'm pregnant."

Every one dropped everything and jumped around her, kissing and embracing her. Aden was moved to tears and started trembling, without being able to say a word, until he managed to whisper:

"Say it again."

"I'm pregnant, my love."

"Again."

"Aden, please compose yourself; you heard me, I'm pregnant and we'll have a baby."

He took her in his arms and kissed her passionately with all the love of his heart; nothing in the whole world could make him happier and no love in the whole world could be greater than he felt then.

The following month, Aden was invited to play Chopin's *Concerto No. 1* with the Warsaw Symphony Orchestra. It was a great honor attributed to him, considering that Poland was Chopin's homeland where all the prestigious competitions in honor of the great composer took place. Carole and Richard decided to accompany him for such a special event, when Edna suggested:

"My opinion would be that Carole should stay home, given her condition, when she doesn't need any excitement or change in schedule."

"I would very much like to go," Carole replied, "considering that this is a very rare musical event and it is a great honor for Aden to perform with the Warsaw orchestra."

Edna did not insist and the three of them flew to Warsaw where they were to stay for a week. In the same time, Edna had finished a commissioned picture and delivered it at the price she had asked for; she had learned long ago not to be modest any more in her negotiations, especially with rich people. She had decided to take a break, until her family will return home; she spent more time reading, listening to music, and watching television. Every day she communicated with the three of them, talking in turn with each who had much to tell about everything that was spectacular in that great city of Poland. There was no time difference between Paris and Warsaw so they didn't have to worry about the calling hour.

One late afternoon, Richard called saying that Aden gave a magnificent performance, and they were on the way to the airport to take the evening flight home; they will see each other in few hours.

Edna called the Benoit family and together they talked a lot about the trip of the three ones and waiting for their return that evening. Suddenly, the television program was interrupted by a special report:

"The plane from Warsaw to Paris had crashed over the Sudetes Mountains, and there were no survivors." Edna had a black mist in front of her eyes, she felt a flash in her brain, and she collapsed with complete loss of awareness. The phone kept ringing but she couldn't hear it anymore. The Benoit family had managed to contact Warsaw airport and Carole, learning that they had been late and missed the plane to Paris. The three of them tried in vain to communicate with Edna and reassure her that they were alive, but her phone did not answer. Richard asked the Benoits to go to the house and see what had happened; in case Edna didn't answer, they should call the police and eventually break down the door and look around the house. The Benoit couple left together, but to no avail, about Edna's fate. They called the police, managed to enter the house and found her unconscious on the floor. Despite all the attempts, they failed to make her revive. The paramedics came immediately, and at the emergency, doctors and nurses surrounded her and made their first attempts to restore her to consciousness, but without success. Edna was wrapped around with tubes and wires connected to all sorts of devices that measured her vital signs. An hour later the doctor told the Benoits who were anxiously awaiting news and who in the meantime had communicated with Richard and informed him about Edna's situation.

"Her vital signs are normal", the doctor said, "but she seems to have suffered a strong shock that blocked her consciousness; she is in a coma and under constant surveillance. For now, that's all I can tell you. We do not yet know how long this state of hers will last; it all depends on the severity with which her mind was touched. You can go home, because I don't see any change in the next few hours and maybe days."

Richard and Aden were devastated, while Carole cried all the time. Directly from the airport, they went to the Benoits house, to find more details about Edna, and left Carole to live with her parents for the time being. From there, they rushed to the hospital, where the doctor repeated what they already knew.

"Can we see her?", Richard asked.

"You can, but she is in a coma, and she will not respond. You also, can try talking to her, and maybe her subconscious will receive some faint signals of your voice connected to bits of events that her brain could bring up to her memory. Sometimes, and I don't say always, this therapy might work; the human brain is a miraculous device that science knows little, close to nothing about the mysterious ways of its functions."

Richard was ready to go inside, when Aden said:

"I can't bear to see her lying there, without talking, without laughing, without moving with her tireless vivacity. You go if you can see her; I can't."

"Sit down and listen. She's lying there only because she thought the two of us died on the plane that crashed. Think of all that she has done for both of us in her life, and how she has always been there for us, with love, care, work, and sacrifices from which she has never ran away. You had no worries to fear, or needs that she did not fulfill for you; you never knew what it meant not to be able to achieve something you wanted, only because she did everything right for you without sparing any effort no matter how hard it was; she was always there for you so that you could grow away from suffering and hardship. Life is not always very easy as you think and many times on its way, we encounter precipices, and difficulties hard to pass. Your mother is the most wonderful person I have ever met. She and I have always been very close to each other, with love, warmth, and mutual trust.

We had hardship, great worries, unforeseen fears, and weak hopes for a bright future; but, together we passed over them and protected you from any troubles that might have come your way; we have built for you a solid foundation on which you can confidently step forward on your own. She has been with you since you were born and guided with her love your steps on a smooth path, to be without difficulties; she built the bond between you two to be indestructible and raised for you the path towards a bright future to live it to the fullest, with happiness and success. Ever since I know her, she has been modest, considerate, and trustworthy, and she has never asked for anything other than to be happy with you and me. The time has come for us both to show her that we are close to her, that we are here for her, and that we love her dearly, especially now that this misfortune has hit her so hard, and as I mentioned before, since it was because of us. Let's go inside."

They both entered the room where Edna was lying unconscious. At the door, Aden stopped without being able to take a step, while heavy tears began to flow down his cheeks. Richard, who was not in a better condition, found a little courage, and pushed him from behind, saying:

"Take that chair and sit next to your mother; hold her hand and start talking. I will stay on the other side."

Aden did what his father told him, and with great difficulty gathered a few whispered words, with which he tried to describe pleasant moments spent some time ago. Now and then, Richard interrupted him, intervening with memories that he had lived with Edna and that brought nostalgic moments in his memory. Despite their best efforts, Edna had shown no sign of life during the time when Richard and Aden had been trying to wake her from the state of unconsciousness. It was late in the evening, when they were both tired and on the doctor's advice, they went home, full of worries and without any hope of improving the situation. Early in the morning, they were both back at their places on either side of Edna.

For ten days and sometimes at night, Richard and Aden sat beside her, holding her hand and talking about everything that went through their memory, only in the hope that the voice of one or the other would break through the mist that covered her mind. From time to time, they took a short break for a cup of coffee, only when the doctor and nurses had to fulfill their duty.

That night, Edna felt a wave of warmth in her hands, but she didn't move. Her eyes were closed and a thick fog in which small-condensed particles that were constantly changing their outline wandered from one end to the other in her field of view. Very slowly, fragments of different shades in intensity began to approach each other, taking on forms of vague significance. Silhouettes without face, with thin bodies outlined by long, black dresses began to move like ghosts that appeared for one moment and disappeared in the next one. A room without ceiling, full of kneeling silhouettes appeared as an image in which deathly stillness predominated the surroundings. In the moments that followed, the whole frame had changed, and things without any connection among them appeared unfolded like a parade of blurred shapes in the fog that prevented the clarity of the vision of their contours and images. From an unknown depth, a faint sound with interruptions of complete silence pierced the fog that had begun to dissipate into small fragments with a decrease in intensity. Vaguely and uncertainly, fragments of feelings appeared in her confused mind, trying to make their way to consciousness. She could see her hand holding the brush with which she was trying to render shapes and contours of images that did not end in concrete subjects; she had the feeling of not being able to concretize lines and shapes that she had conceived as a pictorial achievement barely remembered. The brush seemed to move by itself on the canvas in strokes of colored shades, expressing disparate thoughts and feelings, unrelated to each other, like a self-portrait of her troubled soul. She was struggling in a state of semi-consciousness to find a way to understand what she was feeling, and an explanation for the contoured bits of shapes that loomed before her eyes. With great difficulty the thought of belonging to someone and to a place, crept into her mind; she remembered the fear she once had of being without roots and without having a place in her life where to belong. The fog in her mind began to dissipate, letting her thoughts and feelings pass unhindered into the state of consciousness that had begun to clear. She remembered that she had experienced all the nuances of feelings from the deep darkness of hatred and anger, to the path of the bright light of love, and beauty; she learned them all; she knew them all; she lived them all. The most awful memory that suddenly came to her mind was the feeling of falling into a precipice where the shades of the wind swept away all the feelings she had before, leaving only one, that of belonging nowhere, and which was the shade of non-existence.

Edna opened her eyes and let out a terrifying scream of horror, bursting into tears. Suddenly came into her mind the terrible news that had been told about the plane crash, after which she remembered nothing. The nurse rushed through the door, picked her up in her arms and tried to calm her down, telling her:

"They both are alive; they missed the plane; your son and your husband both live. They stood by you for days and sometimes at nights without moving, holding your hands and talking to you all the time. They are both exhausted and the doctor sent them home. Did you understand what I told you?"

Edna couldn't stop crying, not being sure of what the nurse just said, but slowly her cry became mixed with an immense joy.

"If what you told me is true, I will live. If they died, I would die too. I can't and don't want to live without them."

"They'll both be here like every early morning."

After a little while, Aden and Richard were in her arms, all three crying with sighs of happiness.

"Take me home where I belong."

The shades of bright colors, of harmonious melodies, and of the beauty of the mind and soul prevailed.